KNIGHTS OF THE IMMORTALS

NOBLE TRANSITION

BY CATRINA TAYLOR

Knights of the Immortals
Noble Transition

Written by Catrina Taylor
Digital Version Cover art by Sami Miko
Cover Design by The Writing Network

Midnight Rose
copyright 2015, 2016
ISBN 978 1 63310 0350

Thank you in advance for your review.

Other Books By Catrina Taylor

Xarrok Novels

Birth of an Empire Series

    The Beginning

    Consequences

    Homecoming

    The Fall

Xarrok Origin Stories

    By Flame

    Through Anguish

    Mind Tricks

    Below the Surface

    Change by Design

Xarrok Saga One through Five

Knights of the Immortals

    Knight's Apprentice

    The Choosing

Catrina Taylor

Noble Transition

Chapter 1

James stands inside the house of Clayton Blocc. He's in his jeans. His hair has been trimmed again to conceal his ears. His arm is in a sling. His dark t-shirt and usual tennis shoes echo the world above, but his mind lingers on the events of the last few days.

When his knight appears on the stairs above the foyer, his heart sinks. She stands next to the towering werwolf Journ. His gestures are gentle and she is consumed by his attempt to speak her language. The closer they come to James, the more he feels his stomach knot. He turns his head away from the image to find Councilman Blocc approach him.

"James, I will tell you this, sometimes you don't like what you see, but what you see will help you understand what's most important." Clayton Blocc pats the boy on the shoulder.

"Once you know it's important, then learn how to value it, and share in it, until better times come. Don't want to miss a moment of what matters most, just because what you see isn't what makes you happy." His eyes drift to his daughter and the wolf. "Sometimes it has to be what makes them happy."

James nods. "Yes, sir."

Councilman Blocc pats his shoulder. "You'll understand in time." His voice changes tone. "Ready, Cerita?"

"Yes, Dad." She looks up at Journ. "Catch you on the intergalatic web." She smiles and bounces over to James and her father. "Ready."

Clayton Blocc extends his arm, a light emits from his wrist cuff, and a portal opens feet from him. "You did say you're parked outside the training facility, right?"

James nods with his free hand stuffed deep into his pockets.

Cerita looks at the way the elf is standing. He seems uncomfortable to her, and while she believes she knows why, talking about it isn't something she's ready to do. "My sword? Bag?"

James nods his head toward a pile near the wall.

She gathers her things and puts them over her shoulder. Her new sword weighs her down a bit, but she doesn't allow it to become obvious as she makes her way back to her dad and James. "You sure you're ready for this, Dad?"

"It's long overdue. Let's just hope she's not carrying a frying pan when she sees me." He sighs and extends his arm. "After you."

Cerita steps through and finds herself inside the training facility. When James comes through the portal after her, he walks by without a word. Just before he opens the door, she calls to him, "James . . ."

He stops, looks at her, and waits in silence. His good arm rests on the door.

"What . . ." She pulls her brow tight. "Will I see you tomorrow?"

"We've got school, so yeah."

"And after?"

He shrugs. "Guess not. We've got the rest of the week off training." He lifts his arm in the sling.

As the councilman steps through, he suggests, "Swing by the house on Friday night. I plan to take the two of you to dinner to celebrate without the formality."

He nods. "Yes, sir."

"Good man. I'll see you Friday night." Clayton turns to Cerita. "Our ride should be here in a moment."

She nods, shifts the weight of her sword and bag, then moves for the door. By the time she reaches for it, James is pulling away. She hangs her head. His discomfort bothers her more than she can understand why.

Clayton approaches her, "You know you'll have a long time to sort out your teenage communication issues with your guide, right?"

"Yeah, Dad."

"You're also aware you're both dealing with stuff after this weekend, right?" He looks up as a long black vehicle pulls up to the curb. "Ah, our ride is here."

Cerita believes she should feel impressed by the limousine, but her mind is stuck on her friend, her guide, James. Something's changed and she's struggling to know what to do about it all. The driver holds the door open for her while she places her things on the seat before being reminded to climb in herself. Her dad follows, and the driver closes the door.

Noble Transition

The ride to her house is quiet. Limited small talk surfaces a few times, but with each one lost in thought there is almost no conversation. Both father and daughter fidget. Their eyes drift out the nearest window. When they pull onto her road, Cerita breaks the silence. "You ready?"

He sighs. "No. It's too late to change my mind at this point."

She shrugs. "Could always port to a hotel."

He chuckles nervously. "That'll just make this longer and harder later." He pauses. "Do I look okay?"

Cerita smiles. "Yes, Dad. You look fine. Suit, tie, pants, and shoes. Check. Check. Check. Check. Hair on head? Check." She winks.

He runs his hand through his hair. "I'm so glad this is still mine."

She leans forward as the driver stops the car. "So am I." She tugs on a longer piece next to his ear. "Carlos would look bad bald."

His eyes come to life at the sound of his son's name.

The door opens, she gathers her things, and steps out. Her father follows, but stops at the walkway. "It's . . . I remember when we moved in here." His eyes begin to glisten.

"I usually go in the kitchen door." She treks around to the side of the house, and the side door bursts open as her little sister runs to her.

With her arms flailing, Carolina yells, "Sissy!"

She kneels and scoops up her sister. "Missed you too, Sissy." Little arms wrap around her neck tightly. Cerita looks over her shoulder to see her dad moving slowly, but finally coming up the walk.

Carolina asks, "Who's that, Sissy?"

"He's coming for dinner. Is that okay with you?"

The little girl squints her eyes like she's sizing him up. Then she looks at Cerita. "He looks like Carlos."

"Does he now? Does that mean it's okay for him to come for dinner then?"

The little girl shakes her head intentionally flailing her pig tails so they smack Cerita in the face. Then she says, "Yes."

The girls laugh together. "Well, you've got two who approve of dinner arrangement," Cerita calls as she finally opens the door.

Mom is standing at the stove, finishing with her chicken. When Cerita carries in Carolina, Carmen stops and moves to hug her daughters. "It is wonderful to have you home, mi hija."

Cerita pushes them both further inside the door. "Mama, did you make extra? I invited someone for dinner."

Carmen pinches her brow. "Cerita, you know better than to invite people without talking to me."

"I know, Mama, but this is kinda special." Cerita chews the inside of her lip as she puts her sister on the ground. "Could you get Carlos for me?" Carolina bounces out of the kitchen with excitement.

"What makes this special?" The woman crosses her arms and scowls at her daughter.

"Well, I guess I should have him," stopping mid-thought, she opens the screen door. "Dad."

Carmen's mouth drops. Clayton steps in the side door and their eyes meet. An instant uncomfortable silence settles between them.

"Right. I should go." Cerita meanders out of the kitchen, but turns her head when she hears a crack of skin against skin.

Clayton stands there, looking at Carmen. The smack resonates, and Clayton is left with a stinging reminder of his poor timing on his cheek. Tears fill his eyes as she scolds him for leaving and for coming back, and for breathing in general. He remains silent, listening to everything Carmen says. He doesn't argue with her, or say anything while she continues to berate him. Tears fall freely down his cheeks.

Cerita hangs her head and steps through the threshold to the hallway.

Carlos puts his hand on her arm. "Is that really Dad?"

"Yep. He was at the competition."

"You forgave him?"

"Yep."

The boy looks at the man in the kitchen holding his mother and sobbing on her shoulder. He nods. "Might be hard, but if you can, I can."

The week that follows passes quickly. Many nights are spent in long discussions with very little sleep, but by Friday much is understood. Friday morning, Clayton hands Carmen a credit card with instructions to take Carolina shopping for a dinner dress, and to a hair appointment he's already arranged for them.

While Carmen is spending time with Carolina and Cerita is in school, he takes Ciro shopping. First they find dress attire for their late evening celebration, and then they go car shopping. Clayton is determined that the car Carmen has been stuck driving isn't the one he'll leave behind when he has to return to the city below the sea. Around midday he picks Carlos up early from school. By the end of school, a new car is purchased outright, and he drives it to the high school to pick up Cerita.

As she comes near the car, her eyes grow big. "Dad, where did you get this?"

He smiles. "The dealership down the road." He tosses her the keys. "It's yours. You're going to need it when I am able to convince mom to come home with me."

Carlos leans out the window. "Dad says we all get to move too. Well, except you. He said you did something in the city that doesn't let you leave."

Cerita nods, and then looks down at the keys in her hands. "Yeah, I did something." Her eyes move back to her dad. "I don't get this. Where is all of this coming from? You don't even use money like this back home."

"No, we don't. Our house is addressed differently there, but you know that. Here, there is a small company that works in tech upgrades to established inventions. I own it, privately. We do pretty well. You may have heard of it. It's not far from here." Dad winks.

Cerita's eyes open wider."Thenbold? You own Thenbold?"

He nods. "I'm the silent financier for the company."

Cerita rocks on her feet. "Wow."

He tilts his head. "What?"

"Well, that just leaves a lot of gaps and other stuff in mind." She waves her hand, dismissing much of her immediate disappointment. "But that's the past."

"Well, we need to get you to the mall. You need a new outfit for tonight." He opens his daughter's driver's side door. "Let's get going."

Cerita slides into the car, drops her book bag on the back seat next to Carlos, and slips her keys into the ignition. The car fires up and falls silent while running. She can't remember the last time she's driven a car that ran this quiet. When the door closes on her passenger side, she looks at her dad. "You sure about all of this?"

"Yes." He gestures outward. "Drive."

Carlos sits forward in the back seat. "Come on already. Dad's got other stuff for tonight too."

Cerita rolls her eyes at them both, and slowly pulls through the high school parking lot. Just before turning out onto the main road, she slows to a crawl when she sees James talking to Jenna. His face is taut, and even when Jenna waves at her, he doesn't look her way. She shrinks in the chair before finally pulling into traffic.

Out of the corner of her eye, she sees her dad start to work with a cuff he's put on. Her focus remains on the road, but her mind fixates elsewhere. Carlos starts yammering on about something in school.

Normally, Cerita is interested in what her brother has to say. Today, she can barely hear him.

For every class they are in together, James sat on the far side of the room. Over lunch, he meditated near the woods. In the halls, if he made eye contact, he quickly diverted his gaze elsewhere. He's avoided her their return from the Choosing. Her stomach churns, and her mind attempts to think of one time this week where he actually spoke to her. Or looked at her for that matter. She can't find one.

Tires squeal. Horns blare. Yelling starts. Cerita looks at the light above her, realizing it was red when she passed through it. Her heart skips a beat, and beads of sweat form on the back of her neck. Once they are safely through the now crowded intersection, she exhales audibly. "I'm so, so, so sorry. Is everyone okay?"

Carlos leans back in the seat he's strapped into. "Yep."

Her dad calmly responds, "You're fine. Just turn into the parking lot and park. We're here anyway."

She listens to his instruction, shaken by the experience. Once she is standing outside the car, she leans forward on the roof, and takes measured breaths to calm herself. "So, that wasn't how the first drive in my new car should end."

Carlos climbs out and urges, "Come on. Let's get moving or it'll be midnight dinner." He starts for the nearest mall entrance. Cerita and their father follow him closely.

The next hour passes quickly as Carlos picks out a dress outfit, and has his hair cut. When he is staring in the mirror at his spiked tips, he tilts his head a little, and narrows his eyes.

"Out with it." Cerita stands nearby, watching him. "What do you think? What are you thinking?"

A sly grin perks up his cheeks as he turns to their dad. "Do you think green tips would be too much?"

Clayton shrugs his shoulders. "Not a problem." He gestures to the hair dresser. "Would you be alright tipping it green?"

The plump, dark haired Asian woman smiles brightly. "I think that would be fun." She moves to the back of the room and begins going through cabinets. It only takes her a few minutes to gather supplies.

The whole time the woman is mixing the color, Cerita shakes her head. "I can't believe he's doing this."

Clayton places a hand on his daughter's shoulder. "What's wrong?"

"Mom's going to flip."

He grins. "She's going to have a lot of reason to smile tonight too. I think she'll let me get away with this one." His eyes twinkle as he speaks.

Cerita's eyebrow shoots up at the same time another hair dresser taps her on the shoulder. "I guess I'm waiting for *that* explanation."

Clayton winks as she's directed away.

The stylist puts her into a chair in front of a sink so she can lay backwards to have her hair washed. As the warm water rinses the last of the shampoo out, she receives a text message from Jenna. Once she's able to sit up again, she reads it.

'We need to talk.'

Concerned, Cerita responds, 'What's wrong?'

The stylist moves her to another chair. After wrapping the cloth over her shoulders, the woman pulls her hair out, and begins to trim the ends. Another message comes in, and Cerita is careful to put her phone at eye level so she can read it without being difficult. 'It's James. He's heading back to the city. His arm isn't healing.'

Cerita uses her thumb to respond, 'Why hasn't he said anything? They'll get him fixed there at least.'

As soon as she hits send, another message appears from Jenna. 'He's going to have his aunt treat it.'

Cerita scowls. The hairdresser scolds her for moving so much. Her father comes up to them.

"Cerita, I'm going to take Carlos down to the jewelry store on the first level near where we came in. Meet us there when you're done."

Cerita nods. "Sure, Dad."

The stylist gently scolds her for moving again.

Cerita turns to her as her dad and brother disappear into the crowds beyond. "Can I do just one more thing? Please?"

The older woman laughs. "Of course. Are we doing anything special with your hair today?"

While typing another message to Jenna she shakes her head. "Just pull it back or something. Dad's got some kind of surprise dinner plans or something."

The woman nods. "Alright then."

15

Cerita's back and forth messaging with Jenna keeps her distracted through various pulling, tugging, and combing until the woman spins the chair around so she's facing the mirror again. Her hair has a braid long braid from right to left and around the base of her head. Her long hair rests outside of the circular, crowning braid. She blinks. It takes a moment for her to recognize herself in the reflection.

"You like it?" The woman leans her head next to Cerita's.

Slowly she nods, "Yes. I guess I just have to get used to this."

"To being beautiful? I would think you're already used to that, Miss." The woman spins her around. "Your dad has already paid for your nails to be done as well. Sit tight and we'll have you all set in just a few moments."

"My nails?" Cerita looks down at her hands. The nails are clean, and cuticles are pushed back or gone. "I didn't think there was anything wrong with them."

The woman laughs. "We'll handle it all."

Bewildered, Cerita follows the instructions as the woman, and two others bring a large bucket, a rolling tray, and assorted water bowls, lotions, and tools over. They work to shape, trim, and then color the nails on her hands while her feet are soaking. Then, after moisturizing her feet, shaping her nails, they color them to match her fingers. The glossy finish takes time to dry, but the pampering leaves her feeling uncomfortable in her own skin.

By the time her toes are dry and sneakers are on, she's surprised by how late it's gotten. "Oh, no."

"Everything okay?"

She nods. "Yes. Just need to hurry downstairs."

She flies through the halls, down the stairs, and into the jewelry store. Crossing the threshold, she's not surprised to find the only people in the store are her father and brother. Dad holds a small bag, and her green-tipped, spiky-haired brother stands next to him with a cheesy grin. "What are you two up to?"

Carlos responds in the typical, annoying, little-brother-knows-something-you-don't voice. "Nothing."

Clayton laughs. "It's a surprise for your mom. You look really nice."

"Yeah. This is a bit much for me." She lifts her fingers and turns them while wiggling them for him to see. "I'm not built like this."

He grins. "Sure you are. You just don't know it yet."

She shakes her head. "We done?"

"Yes. Your outfit is waiting back in your room." Her dad gestures for the door. "Let's get going."

The drive home is much smoother than the drive in was. When they get into the house, she notices her mother and baby sister have had the same pampering she has had. Her father lavishes her mother with compliments, and kisses. After his affectionate greeting, he turns to Cerita. "You ready?"

She shrugs. "I guess. You said my outfit was in my room, right?"

He laughs. "Yes, but not this room."

Her eyes grow wide. "Oh." Her eyes cut to her mom, and then Carlos. "Ah um, she's aware?"

"Somewhat. It's time to make everything understood." He smiles, extends his free hand, while holding his wife in his other arm. "We've been talking about this all week. I hope you're ready to see it all."

Her mother looks up at him. "You want me to believe your fairy tales?"

He leans over and places light kisses against her face as he's speaking, "The same ones I tried to share with you all those years ago."

She laughs. "Alright. Come on. Show me the magic."

He chuckles. "Nothing magic about any of it." He glances back to Cerita. "Grab the sword."

Her mother's eyes grow wide in surprise. "Sword? There is a sharp weapon in my home? A sword?"

Cerita hangs her head, traipses into her room, grabs her sword bag, and slings it over her shoulder. When she returns to the living room, her mother's stern expression knots her stomach. "Yes, Mom. My sword."

Clayton explains, "It was mine, but it was time to pass it on."

The woman crosses her arms and scowls at her eldest. Clayton kisses Carmen's frown lines and the deep creases in her scowl.

It's a fight against her husband's affection to remain upset at her daughter. She extends a stern finger toward her daughter. "This isn't over with, young lady."

He kisses her mouth, lingering to hold her attention, and when the children groan, she pulls away and laughs. "Stop this. You had magic to show me, right?"

He laughs. "No. You've spun the magic. What I'm going to do is show you the technology."

Cerita gathers Carolina into her arms and holds Ciro's hand as her father extends his free arm. A bright light floods the room, and the portal shifts through the stages to the stable purple and black spiral she's become accustomed to. Cerita looks over at Carmen for a reaction.

Mom gasps.

Carolina peeks up from the inside of her neck. "Pretty. Purple, like my dress." She pats the lower part of her little gown proudly.

Carlos exclaims, "Oh, cool!"

Ciro steps hesitantly toward the portal. He stops short of the threshold and looks up at his big sister.

Cerita nudges them forward. "It's safe. Go on."

He looks up at her with large round eyes, but says nothing. His eyes divert to the portal again and he takes a deep breath.

"We'll go together." She smiles, holds his small hand in hers, and the three siblings walk through.

Clayton holds onto his wife's hand tightly. "Come on. Need to see where the kids went right?"

Carlos yells as he's going through, "I'm first!"

"I'm not sure." Carmen hesitates her steps, withdraws her hand, covers her mouth with it. "They're okay?"

"They are fine. They're on the other side. They are in our home, if . . ." He searches her eyes. "you want it to be."

She tilts her head slightly, slides her hand into his, and squeezes it. Exhaling carefully before they step through together. The sight on the other side of the purple spiral takes the woman by surprise.

"Clayton, it's beautiful!" Carmen's eyes search the elaborately designed room they arrive in.

"Not as beautiful as its mistress." His kisses his wife on the cheek. "We have so much more to see, but first I need to speak with the staff about dinner."

Her eyes widen. "Staff?" She glances around again at the elaborate room. Extending her arm toward the room, she gushes, "I suppose one would be needed for a place this large. There's no way I could keep up on it all."

"If I have my way, you'll never have to lift a finger to do anything you don't want to, ever again." He places a hand over his wife's as she loops it through his arm. With a warm smile and gentle conversation, he leads her through the house and to the kitchen before taking her on a grand tour of the compound. Ciro and Carolina follow through the tour, and chatter about the sights they encounter as Clayton explains it's all available to them.

** *** **

Carlos follows Cerita up the grand staircase to the next floor, and down the hallway to the second door on the left. The windows they pass are larger they he is, and he comments on it. Cerita just smiles at him. He steps into her suites and races for the balcony on the other side of the first room they step into. "Wow. This place is huge."

"Yep. The house, the grounds, even the city." Cerita drops her bag on the bed and moves out with her brother. She leans over the balcony and looks out over it. "There's so much I didn't see while I was here last week. Maybe we can walk around together or something."

"What? Being seen with your brother won't cramp your cool style?" He pokes her in the ribs.

"Eh, only if you plan to be a dweeb."

"What who you're calling a dweeb, dingbat." He laughs and she laughs with him. "So, you have any idea why he didn't help all these years?"

"Not a clue." The mood sombers. "Wish I knew, but if we keep looking for that kind of stuff, we aren't going to enjoy what's happening now." She pauses, looks at her brother, "At least that's what mom would say."

"Yeah, she would. She's been really happy this week too. Guess they really still love each other, hu?"

Cerita nods. "Yeah. A lot." She steps back toward her rooms. "You want to raid the kitchen? You could almost get lost in it." She pauses, then adds, "No, you could get lost in it."

Carlos's eyes grow large at the prospect. "Lead the way."

** *** **

James settles against a large chair as several elf men and women blend together the ingredients of a rub that will take away the ache associated with the repairs in his arm. He tries to focus his thoughts for meditation but finds himself lacking the self-discipline. Typically he would dismiss it, but this time he knows what has him distracted is something that can't be easily ignored. It has been eating into his thoughts all week, and has grown to the point that he's struggling now.

His aunt enters the room with a tall, young elf woman. Her hair is long and full of curls, her eyes are a soft blue, and clothing is thinly draped over her. She folds her hands together and remains behind his aunt.

Vivian checks on the salve, and dismisses those working on it. "Remove your shirt."

James complies.

Vivian steps near her nephew and begins to rub the salve into his shoulder and arm. While she works, she watches his reactions.

He leans back while his aunt rubs the mixture into his arm. Closing his eyes, he fights the image of his knight being kissed by the vampyre again. His thoughts urge him to balance his view, but his heart tugs him in another direction.

Vivian finishes rubbing from shoulder through his wrist. "You are Guide, my nephew. You are also my heir. There are certain privileges afforded you at this junction in your life. She who will remain nameless stands before you. She comes of the dark elves to serve the heirs and family."

His eyes open suddenly, and he looks at her. His brothers had told him of some of the privileges afforded to elves of different statures, but this one he always ignored. "I don't require services."

"Do not question my judgment." Vivian narrows her eyes. "She is here to provide the needed mental focus, James. Do not assume I would encourage behaviors that would lead to defilement of our line." Her voice is unusually terse.

"Of course." His face warms. His eyes drop. "Forgive me, Aunt Vivian."

"You are young. Do not repeat such assumptions. You have an appointment this evening in the house of our next emperor. You will be at your best. She will be here to help you prepare, first your mind, and then your attire." Vivian looks at the young woman. "Traditional dress for a ceremony, although one will not be encountered this day."

The young woman nods her head. "As you wish, Eldress."

Vivian's eyes narrow upon the young woman. "Do not become temptress, or you shall be sent to the mainland."

"It is my wish to serve the house of Sáralondë."

"Good." Vivian turns to her nephew again. "Refocus your thoughts. Learn what she can teach you, as you do yourself and your knight no justice by your behaviors of late."

"Yes, Aunt Vivian." He never knows how she is aware of his actions on the mainland below, but he never questions her methods either. She is usually right, even when admitting it means he's caused problems.

As his aunt leaves them alone, the young woman urges him from the seat. "Please, sire, find your meditation position."

"One, *do not* call me sire. Ever. That *does not* apply." He lifts two fingers and continues in a terse tone. "Two, I reach meditation in any position I chose." He sighs and relaxes. "I've never needed a ritual, simply silence." He slumps back into the chair. "But lately my mind races in silence."

The elven girl folds her hands together and kneels in front of the guide. "Then you need a new focus. It is far easier than you may realize, yet takes great concentration for one so troubled."

"What makes you think I'm troubled?"

Her soft blue eyes drift to meet his as she responds. "Guide, you chastised me for a simple slip of the tongue, and you are tense. It takes very little to see that your mind is troubled."

He leans forward on his knees, and rubs his face with his hands. In a much calmer tone he asks, "What do you suggest?"

"There are several things to bear in mind. For now, let us find the simplest. Perhaps a sound that calms you? Or a single item for focus?"

He shakes his head. "Sounds don't work like that for me."

"Then an item it is." She smiles, shifts carefully so her hair remains covering areas of concern, and she retrieves a candle from the shelves in the room. Once it is lit, she places it on the floor by his feet. She kneels on both knees, and looks at the flame. "Focus on the flame. Do not wander from the fire. A thought that moves into your mind or a distracting image, allow the heat of the flame to consume it."

He stares into the flame and struggles against the images his mind often recalls in moments of quiet. Taking the girl's advice, he imagines the heat of the flame consuming the image like an old photo burning to ash. His concentration wavers less the longer he focuses.

It isn't until a hand rests on his bare arm that his mind returns to the moment. He exhales slowly, grateful for the relief. His eyes wander up toward the young woman. "Thank you."

"Of course. Your celebration attire has been laid upon the bed. Do you require assistance putting it on?"

He lifts an eyebrow. "No. I can manage." Moving to his feet, he realizes he's not much taller than she is.

"As you wish. Will you require food or drink?" She holds both hands together in front of herself.

He dismisses the suggestion with a shake of his head. "I believe they are serving dinner in the house of Blocc."

She lowers her head. "That is my understanding too. I shall leave you now. Your aunt requires my aid."

James waits for the woman to exit his family's home before moving to his bedroom to prepare. Spread on the bed is a tunic that closes in the front, and long slacks. Being the first event he's been told to wear this ceremonial garb, he tries to recall every aspect of the symbolism involved in the design.

The color of the tunic and slacks match the sky blue of the elven crest. The cover for his boots resembles the deep brown color of the Earth, and everything that holds it together is the dark blue of night. Nothing missing. All three aspects of the elven tribe are represented in crucial ways. The foundation of a man is in his feet. He embodies his people, where they begin, and holds them together in light or dark.

With a heavy sigh and his stomach churning, he mutters to himself, "I can't believe all of this thought went into one outfit."

He pulls the tunic over his shoulders, then ties it in the front. "Buttons would be an improvement." He pulls the pants up so they rest at his waist. The pull string is secured. He readjusts the tunic, and then slides on soft shoes with the covers over them, instead of his usual boots. The ground feels odd beneath his feet. Stepping before a full length mirror, he finger combs his hair into some semblance of acceptable.

His eyes catch movement in the peripheral. He turns his head to find nothing. "Great. Now I'm seeing things."

"What are you seeing, Guide?" The gentle voice of the elf woman sent to help him carries from behind.

He spins, squares himself with her, and stares. "Don't creep behind me, or anyone for that matter."

She lowers her head, and her hair falls forward. "Do forgive my poor decision. I move lightly, and do not recall announcing myself each time I enter a room."

He waves his hand. "Don't do it again. What do you need?"

She extends a wreath of laurel leaves. Her eyes remain diverted from his face as she lifts it higher. "It is the Sky Crown. You represent our people this evening. It is wise to wear it."

He extends his hand, taking the leaf crown from her. Looking it over slowly leads his stomach to churn. "This is not my place. I do not hold such a position for our people. I simply guide Earth's knight." His hand returns the crown. "Please return this to the Eldress of Peace."

She nods. "As you wish, Guide. The elven attire is appealing on you." She half smiles from one side before nibbling on her lower lip. "I will go now."

He turns away from her, and hears the door close a few moments later. He collects his cuffs, and guide technology into his leather bag.

Once he's content with his essentials, he gathers two more specialized bolts for his crossbow. Before closing it, he withdraws his left cuff, then slings the bag over his shoulder. Securing his cuff, he takes a deep breath. "It's a simple recognition ceremony. I do not need to do more than enjoy a meal, and acknowledge what is needed. I can do this."

"Indeed you can, Nephew." The voice of his aunt carries through a side window. "I would not have selected you to attend, if you could not. In time, you will take a more active role representing our people. Tonight is merely the first."

"I know, Aunt Vivian. It feels wrong for me to go without you as lead."

"You are ready for this step." Her tone is emotionless, but her assurance is certain.

He holds his gaze with her. "If you are sure, then I guess I am."

"You have trained all of your life to take the place as heir. You are ready."

"I guess I should go, so I'm not late."

"We will speak again once you are at home with your parents." She moves past the window, leaving him to open his portal.

Noble Transition

Within moments, James stands inside the foyer of the house of Blocc. A servant greets him, then leads him into a room with eighteen chairs around a long table. The room is lit only by candlelight, and emitters that mimic the same. The food is being brought out and placed in the center. While he is not the first to arrive, he is the youngest to represent one of the twelve tribes at this point. The servant escorts him to one of the empty chairs, and fills his chalice with a soft colored liquid.

"Thank you," se says as he's sitting.

"You are welcome, sire." The servant lowers his head, and moves to the next guest, to fill his chalice as well.

Councilman Rol leans toward James, speaking quietly, "That is a term few in the line ever get used to. Even more so when it is merely a formal setting choice, instead of your actual position."

"I didn't realize my dislike was that visible, Councilman."

He laughs heartily. "You should see your features, young elf. You are a transparent kind, unlike your aunt."

"I'll take that to be a compliment." His eyes drift from the councilman to the empty chair at an angle from him. The servant escorts in the vampyric representative. Although James is no longer the only one his age representing his people, he presses his lips into a thin line when his eyes meet Darach's.

"It is good to see you again, Guide." The vampyre's voice carries a tone of superiority. He's dressed in a long black coat over midnight blue dress slacks, and an equally dark colored shirt. As he sits, he shifts his coat to the hands of the servant, who moves quickly out of the room with it.

Rol whispers again to James, "Remember you are transparent."

James clears his throat. "It is good to see you again. I didn't realize you represented the heir."

The vampyre smirks. "I don't. He is offworld, my master suggested I attend in his place. The heir agreed." Darach laughs. "I expect tonight will be interesting."

Councilman Rol raises his glass, "Tonight is about first moments. Let's enjoy your first moments as representatives of your tribes."

Many of those who can hear Rol Shoal also raise their glasses to the boys. The Amazonian representative, responds, "What a tribute it is to see such life among the families. Welcome." She is a young woman, older than the boys, but far from as aged as many of those on the council. Her hair is flaming red, and her voice is soft. She stares directly into James' eyes.

He blushes.

Darach smiles. "Thank you, m'lady." His smile grows when the woman's eyes shift to his own. He sips his drink, but does not break eye contact.

Shoal laughs heartily again. "It seems this young one fancies himself a charming man."

The room laughs with him, and Darach's face warms to a soft red.

A servant interrupts the laughter with an announcement. "Please welcome his future majesty, Clayton Blocc and his companion, Carmen Guzman."

Whispering runs the length of the table, as the representatives all stand for the human tribe leader to enter.

Clayton Blocc enters the room dressed in a deep blue suit with a burgundy dress shirt. His wife enters wearing a burgundy gown. They move together to the head of the table. She fusses with him, as he attempts the formality of the escort.

Carmen turns to see Carolina, and Ciro announced. Carolina waits for no one, but runs to her mom, and throws her little arms around her waist. Carmen scoops up her youngest, and Ciro is shown to his seat. She settles Carolina in the empty chair next to Clayton.

Once the whispers of the cute child subside, the servant announces, "Welcom Carlos Blocc, of the Blocc family line." Carlos, with his green spiked tips, stands in a black and silver tuxedo. His nervous smile paints his face while the servant gestures him forward, and to his chair.

Everyone is quiet one more time when the servant speaks again. "Please welcome the Knight's Apprentice of Earth, Cerita Guzman-Blocc."

Cerita enters the room.

Her hair is curled in ringlets that cascade down the back of her head. The ringlets are framed by the braided crown. The limited makeup on her face enhances the light in her eyes.

Her deep purple gown wraps around her neck at the top, and drops loosely at her sides. While it does not reveal anything, it does hug her natural curves. Without one of her brothers to escort her to the table, the servant does this himself.

Once she is at her chair, she leans slightly toward James, and whispers, "You're blushing, and you should really breathe."

He only nods before he is finally able to force his eyes from her.

Clayton Blocc seats his wife, before sitting himself. Dinner is served, and everyone freely talks among themselves for hours. During this time, James remains quiet, but is unable to keep from stealing glances at Cerita.

Between the meal and dessert, Mr. Blocc stands at the head of the table. Once everyone is quiet, and their attention is focused on him, he pushes his chair back, kneels toward Carmen, and clears his throat. "Years ago, I left this life to make one with you. This life gripped me again and drew me back in, but it's always been incomplete. I've asked you before, but I'm asking again, will you take me as your husband?"

Before he is finished, tears run down her face, and a smile warms her features. "Yes, Clayton."

He slides a small ring on her finger. It begins to glow a soft yellow, then white. He wraps his arms around her waist and lifts her from the chair as he stands. Tears also flow down his face. He buries his head in her neck. "My beautiful, Amazon."

"My Clay." She kisses his cheek.

Carlos leans over toward Cerita. "Told you Dad had stuff for dinner."

Cerita shakes her head.

Desert is served as the happy couple settles again.

Shoal raises his glass, and asks, "When will you have the ceremony?"

Now holding his wife's hand, Clayton looks at her. "When would you like it to be?"

Carmen asks, "Do we have to wait?"

Shoal grins. "I can perform it tonight, if you wish. We have audience with every tribe."

The Amazonian woman, whose name is Vanisha, gestures, "It would take little to confirm the tribal line. We already sent your nanites to the center. Then you could announce your heir tonight after the ceremony."

"I don't know about announcing my heir." Clayton's eyes look between his eldest children. "I want to speak with them first."

"Of course." Vanisha smiles warmly. "Should I check on the data?"

Rol nods, "Of course." He looks to the elf next to him, who also agrees. From there, agreement is passed from one to the other at the table. Vanisha contacts the medical facility to verify the DNA line of the future empress and returns a positive confirmation.

Settling into after dinner conversations in the entertainment room, Vanisha approaches Carmen and Clayton with the results, which confirm the information he's been providing.

"It seems, during his short tenure as Earth's Knight, he was sent to find your parents." She hands a glass of wine to Carmen. "Your line is of that of one of our great generals. She retired to the mainland when she was impregnated, and vanished from our records. I'm pleased to hear she eventually passed without pain."

"Yes. Mom was a great lady. I often miss that she didn't know her grandchildren." Something occurs to Carmen. "Wait. How old do Atlantean Amazons live?"

Vinisha's grin grows. "Well over a century." Vanisha looks to Clayton."I take it you've not told her what her mother's age was, have you?"

"It didn't seem important." He smiles and gazes at the beautiful woman on his arm.

Carmen looks between them. "How old could she have been?"

"She didn't leave Atlantis until she was around one hundred." Vanisha sips her wine slowly. "You grew up with her for a long life."

"I was barely twenty five when I lost her." Carmen glances at Cerita, who's talking to the other knight. "I believe Clay and I had just been married, although Mom insisted she didn't meet with him, now I know why."

He nods. "I had long since given up Atlantis by then, but she would have had no way of knowing it."

"Funny how you gave up Atlantis, and yet here you are serving the dominion with great strength, and looking forward to the Change of Hands." Vanisha lifts her glass.

Clayton pulls Carmen a little closer. "I found something more amazing than I could have imagined." He sighs, looks at Vinisha, "However, duty and responsibility called. The accident hurried things up. Mainlanders would have learned too much all at once. We just aren't ready for that."

"You were looking out for Atlantis all along." Vinisha smiles warmly and lifts her glass. "Seems you never really left here, just found your family."

Carmen looks up into her husband's eyes. "So tell me my love, how old are you? Really?"

He laughs, leans over, and kisses her tenderly before answering, "I will turn sixty five soon."

She laughs. "So, I'm married to an old man?"

He leans over and whispers in her ear, "I'll show you how old after the ceremony."

She quietly squeals and laughs.

Vanisha shakes her head and mutters, "Newlyweds," under her breath.

Rol Shoal calls everyone together. "I ask that we bring everyone here. Please form a circle around the bride and groom." Once a circle of witnesses surround Clay and Carmen, he continues, "Who will stand with you both?"

Carmen looks to Cerita and extends her hand. "My beautiful daughter, Cerita."

Shoal smiles. "And who will stand with you, Clay?"

He chuckles. "If you weren't officiating, I'd have asked you."

Shoal pats his friend on the shoulder. "Well, old man, you should pick another. How about one of the young ones?"

Clay looks over his shoulder toward James, but before he can speak, Darach offers.

"If you would accept me, sire, I would stand with you." Darach bows his head slightly toward Clay, in a formal gesture he places an arm across his abdomen, and one behind in back.

"Oh. Well. Okay then. Come on, Darach." Clay gestures toward the young vampyre. Then he looks at James and shrugs.

James nods, but his eyes drift to Cerita standing next to her mother in the lower lighting of the evening Atlantean skyline. He can feel his heart thumping hard against his chest. When she smiles, he can feel his face blush. He's hardly spoken a word to her, even at the times she's only been inches away from him. Regardless of being unable to speak to her, she hasn't left his mind since she entered the dinner hall.

Shoal begins the vows. "Clayton Blocc, repeat after me, I, Clayton Blocc, love you, Carmen, as I have loved no other. All that I am I share with you. If you will allow it, I take you to be my wife through all that may come, now and forever."

"I, Clayton Blocc, love you, Carmen, as I have no other. All that I am I share with you. If you will allow it, I take you to be my wife through all that may come, now and forever."

Shoal turns to Carmen. "Will you allow him?"

"I will."

"Now, Carmen Guzman, repeat after me. I, Carmen Guzman, love you, Clayton, as I have no other. All that I am, I share with you. If you will allow it, I take you to be my husband through all that may come, now and forever."

"I, Carmen Guzman, love you, Clayton, as I have no other. All that I am, I share with you. If you allow it, I take you to be my husband through all that may come, now and forever."

Shoal turns to Clayton. "Will you allow her?"

"I will."

"Well then, do those standing with them approve?" Shoal looks directly to Cerita.

"I do." Her voice cracks slightly. Her eyes drift between her parents, and then to Darach over her father's shoulder. A half smile is met with one from the vampyre.

"I approve." Each syllable is enunciated carefully by the young vampyre.

The Atlanteans then grasp hands around the four encircled individuals, as the husband embraces his wife tightly and kisses her deeply. A chanted blessing for long life and marriage is spoken by the guests, and the ceremony is over.

As the circle breaks up to congratulate the couple, Darach slips his hand into Cerita's and pulls her from the crowd. When she is near enough to hear him, he whispers closely, "Your parents look wonderful together."

A soft smile decorates her face. "They a really do." She catches sight of her brother, Carlos, sitting alone watching it all. "I should speak with him."

"Mind if I come?" Darach doesn't release her hand right away.

She shrugs. "Sure. If you'd like."

They walk to where Carlos is. She looks for a chair, only to have Darach bring one to her.

She asks, "Everything okay?"

"Yeah. You know, when Dad . . ." He looks at Darach and changes his words. "The start of the week was fun?"

"Yeah. It was." She smiles. "Darach, would you mind excusing us? Please?"

He nods. "As you wish."

Once they are alone, she hugs her brother. "I know this is a lot to take in. I've had just over a month to get used to it all, but I was right where you're at when I started."

"At first the thought of Dad coming home was shocking enough, but to then find out he's loaded on Earth and royalty in Atlantis . . . it's just different."

"Well, we live from Mom's check, to mine, to Mom's to . . ." Cerita sighs. "And then we find out we're not even really like everyone we know. Yeah, it's hard to take in."

"I'm glad Mom and Dad are happy. They look like they never separated over there." His gaze levels with his mom cradled into his father's arm. "And Dad hasn't even blinked at two more kids, but then, why would he when he's loaded?"

Cerita slaps his arm. "He could be like the jerk that left Mom with Ciro and Carolina in the first place, taking all of that money when he left and putting us into the position we have had live with"

Carlos shakes his head. "No. I don't think that's in him." His eyes rest on his dad. "He's actually a good guy, but," he sighs. "I don't know. Just different."

"You're probably right." Cerita also looks over at her parents, who still seem to glow in joy. "So, how are you going to feel coming back and forth to Atlantis on a whim?"

He shrugs. "Not sure yet. I don't really belong here, but then, I do. I don't know."

"Well, we've got a lot ahead to think about. Nothing will ever be the same again."

He looks at his sister. "That's what we thought when Mom got that great new job."

She smirks, and rolls her eyes. "Okay fine. So, it's a lot more than not the same again."

"You think?"

"Yeah, maybe. Just a bit over the top, somewhere." She playfully jabs him in the shoulder.

The siblings laugh together. Cerita gets quiet when James walks by them to the drink bar. Her eyes remain on him as she follows him back with the drinks to the Amazonian, Vanisha.

"So, what's up with you and those two guys? I thought you and James had a thing."

She shrugs. "Not really one of those things that you talk about with your little brother, but we've had some strange things happen lately, so I'll try to. James and I like each other, a lot. But he's my guide. I'm his knight. As a team who have to work together under extreme situations, where life and death could be common place, it's frowned upon for us to be 'that kind of' involved. If something went wrong, it could make things really bad for our assignment. So, we've agreed not to act on liking each other that way."

Her eyes glance back over to him. "But I think I hurt his feelings and I don't know how to fix it."

"Okay. And that vampy boy?"

Cerita gazes at Darach. His hair is neatly styled. He carries himself as a member of the nobility, but when they are together, she knows there's both an edge and a gentleness to him. "I don't know yet."

"He's not James?"

Cerita's eyes dart to Carlos. "Some things take time." She messes with his hair. "You'll figure it out when you're a little older, like twenty eight or something."

They laugh together again, as he dodges her hand.

"I wonder if Ciro and Carolina are actually sleeping or if that servant lady is spoiling them both as she threatened Mom she would do." Carlos looks toward the stairs in the foyer. "You think they are going to be okay with this?"

Cerita nods. "They already seem like they are. Ciro was excited about the new tram to the school."

Carlos laughed. "Yep. He was. Carolina loves the gardens too. I lost her in them this morning."

Cerita's eyebrows shoot up. "You did?"

"Yep. It was funny too. Couldn't find her until the bush laughed at me." Carlos looks over to his sister. "They'll be fine. Won't they?"

"Well, it's getting late. I suppose we could sneak up to find out." Cerita glances past him to the large staircase.

"And get out of the monkey clothing?"

"My thoughts exactly." She giggles and they begin to sneak out of the entertainment room, and into the foyer. When they cross the threshold between the two, a bright light appears as someone opens the portal. In steps Journ. "Carlos, go upstairs. I'll be right behind you. I need to speak to him."

"Another one of your boyfriends?"

She shakes her head. "No. Another knight."

"Ah. Well then. Enjoy slaying dragons or whatever you do." He disappears up the stairs.

She waits until she knows Journ's portal has both closed and her brother is beyond earshot. "How are you?"

The tall werwolf looks at the knight. "Not well. I bring news for those assembled."

"Should I be a part of it?"

He shakes his head. "I am liaison for Rol Shoal. He will make assignments."

She nods. "He is through that doorway."

She indicates how to find Councilman Rol, and makes her way upstairs, expecting to be summoned soon. She prepares her sword, and dagger. Once she adjusts the supplies in her equipment bag, she draws a warm bath.

Before climbing in the tub, she contacts her father who assures her there is nothing to be concerned with.

Once she's back in the bathroom, she finds herself looking in the mirror, taking in the final image of what her look became for the night. "A knight doesn't require all of this, but a princess would." She laments. "I don't want to be his heir."

She sighs heavily and starts to pull the braid out of her hair. As she reaches the last twist, something strikes the bathroom window. She looks towards it, but sees nothing, and she shrugs it off. She starts to put the pins in a container only to hear something strike her window again. This time Cerita walks over to see if anything is outside and is almost struck by a nearly golden, flat training disk. "Hey!"

"Sorry!" Someone calls up from below her window.

She sticks her head farther out so she can see them. "Darach?"

"Yeah. Got a few minutes?"

"It's getting late. Dad said everyone left. I . . ." She sighs. "Sure. But I don't think we should be yelling like this."

"Meet me on your balcony?"

"How are you going to get up here?"

"Just open the doors. I'll see you in a minute."

She shakes her head as she steps back into the bathroom. Grabbing a plush green robe on her way to the door, she ties it tight around her dress, then opens the double glass doors to the larger balcony. Darach is standing on the other side of the door. His hair is a bit tousled, and his usual perfect posture is diminished. "You okay?"

Winded briefly, he nods. When he is standing again, he smiles. "Haven't jumped like that in years."

Cerita's eyes grow wide. "You *jumped*?" His eyes twinkle with pride. "I had no idea you could do that."

He nods. "We're among the strongest on Atlantis." He chuckles. "It's not important. You snuck out of the reception. Everything okay?"

"Yeah." She steps back into her room. "Just needed to get out of the garb."

Darach shrugs off his long jacket and places it on the nearest chair. "It gets old, doesn't it?"

"Yes. It *really* does." She drops into a chair. "I actually like training, fighting James, it's fun trying to knock the master off balance, and trying to keep up with the wolf cubs not far from us is one of the best games ever."

"But all of this ritual stuff sucks." He adds.

"Oh yeah. Big time."

"Eh, you'll get used to it."

"If you grow up with it. Heck, three months ago, I was carrying home groceries that I bought with money from a job my family needed me to keep, just to keep food. Now," she extends her arms, "this."

"You worked, instead of training?" His eyebrows lift high as he leans forward.

"What? Knight is the first job you've ever had?"

"Nope. Trainee was. But then I started a lot sooner than you did." He folds his hands together. "I activated the knight's sword, by accident, at five. Been training ever since."

"Five?"

"Yep. Most knights start training at seven or nine, or something a bit later. But then, most knights don't stumble over a sleeping knight very often, let alone at five." He shrugs. "It was an odd situation. Still is, really."

"I guess we all have an odd story."

"Seems like everyone in the Choosing this year has their own unique tale to tell. You're the one with the most impressive story though. Perfect, little mainlander thrust into our world by mistake. Didn't know who her daddy was, but worked hard anyway. Oh how hard it must have been to work like you have." He mock pouts. "Oh, how desperate it must be."

Cerita glares. "You really have no idea."

"You're right. I don't. The only place on Earth I've ever been is here." He sits taller. "Atlantis is all I've known of the world we come from. A large area as I'm told Atlantis is, I know the planet is much larger. Goblins bring in a lot of the culture from above and I'd like to actually see some of it."

"Why haven't you? You appear to be nobility too. I get the feeling there's freedom in that."

"There is, but then there's not. It's like our training. We learn to fight, and we get pretty good at it. But once we get good enough, there's the Choosing, which leads to our assignments. Then we stick to our planet." He shrugs. "Freedom to beat the life out of something, only to be limited to who we are told that will be."

She shakes her head. "I see it differently. Beating something isn't my goal. We need to be resourceful before we settle on painful."

"We need to get the job done, no matter what the cost."

"We will obviously be doing our job differently."

"I see that." The corners of his mouth slide up slightly. "Guess you've got the royal attitude that I do not. But then it'll be another two thousand years before it matters. My grandchildren will groom the next Vampyric Emperor."

"When does the throne change hands next?"

"Cats hand it to the humans in a few years. Not tomorrow soon, but not far off either." Darach leans back in the chair again. His eyes take in the room. "What do you think of all of this so far? Really think of it?"

"I think there's a lot I don't know and better learn fast." She sighs. "Things I should tell my brothers about or something."

"That sounds about right. Have you had time to actually see the city yet?" He smirks.

"Only from the balcony."

He extends his hand to her. "Come, let's get out of here."

Her face pulls back. "Uht, ah. Not in this dress and robe."

He laughs. "You're beautiful in anything, I'm sure."

"Well, then, let me put on anything else." She smiles, steps into the bathroom, releases the hot water from the tub and slips into jeans and a t-shirt. After pulling her hair into a ponytail, she joins Darach again.

"Wow." His voice seems to soften with each sound.

"What?" Looking at herself trying to find a flaw, she feels confused.

"I was right. You're beautiful in anything."

With her face warm, she drops her eyes. "You really need to stop doing that stuff."

"What stuff? Being honest?"

Her eyes look up to meet his. "Complimenting me. It's just not a thing." She nibbles on the inside of her cheek. "I mean, we are being taught to protect, not . . . date."

His face softens and a smile broadens. "Date? Courting. Is that what we're doing?"

Her eyes widen. "Well, I thought that's what you were trying to convince me to do."

He feels his face warm. "Traditions are very different where we come from. It's not uncommon for Vampyre to have close associations with each other. And I tend to speak what comes to mind, so you hear it as I think it." He looks away from her for the first time. "Dating. Courting is more . . . it's just more."

"Oh. Well, where I come from dating is to find out if we want it to be more." She tilts her head. "What were you hoping with this?"

"I was hoping to make a pretty girl smile. Kinda hoping to learn more about you, and the mainlands, and . . ." He shrugs. "Maybe get a chance for more friends." He pauses long enough to see her face before adding. "Yep. I think it, you hear it."

She laughs. "You seem so much more put together during all the ceremonial events."

"Aren't we all?" He leans his head to the side a little with a slight smile.

"Okay. Good point. Well, can't tell you much about the last part, but I'm up for all the smiling, and learning about each other stuff."

"Do I get to kiss you?"

"Haven't you done that once already?"

He shrugs. "I tried, but hard to kiss a woman who doesn't kiss you back."

"Oh. Well, then . . . We'll have to give it some thought." She smiles. "You were going to show me Atlantis?"

"Let's start with the center city, where you live when you're here. At least for tonight." He smiles warmly and extends his hand to her.

It's early morning before Darach brings her home. Both are so engaged in conversation that they enter through the front door, only to encounter her mother standing in the foyer. The only reason either realize she's staring at them, arms crossed over her chest, is because they nearly run into her. Cerita stops short, and her heart thumps against her chest.

"Mama."

Carmen extends her finger. "Don't 'mama' me, young lady. Where have you been?"

Darach lowers his head. "Please accept my humblest apologies, Your Highness. I had made the promise to show Cerita the city some weeks ago. We were fulfilling that promise, Your Highness. Regretfully, time escaped us." He bows his head and shoulders enough to add to his affectionate term of her position.

She narrows her eyes. There is a long, uncomfortable pause before she finally says, "Don't make it a habit, young man."

"No. Of course not." Darach bows slightly lower. "May this day continue to shine as you do."

Cerita watches him in amusement. Once again, he turns on the charm, and surprisingly it works on her mother.

"Coffee, mi hija?"

Cerita nods. "That sounds wonderful."

Darach stands up straighter. "What is this coffee?"

43

Cerita's smile brightens. "You've never had coffee? The Goblins haven't brought coffee?"

"No coffee." He confirms.

"Oh, well, then we must correct that." Carmen loops an arm around one of Darach's, and with Cerita they escort him into the kitchen, telling him about the joys, preparation, and variations of the warm bitter liquid they are about to indulge in.

** *** **

James throws his legs over the side of the bed, and rubs his face in his hands. At least the ache in his arm is gone, now if he could get the other ache to go away, he'd be content. Although the sun hasn't risen, the cows are starting to stir beneath him. He stands, slides on slippers, and trudges down the ladder to the stalls.

Every morning he's thankful for the Atlantean tech his parents use in the barn. When his nose picks up the scent of cow feces his stomach turns. Every time he descends it hits him. He releases their small herd into the pasture, for the day. Once he's content with the quiet in the barn, he makes his way into the house and kitchen.

First thing James does is open the refrigerator, but his eyes take a few minutes to locate the egg carton. He pulls the whole thing from the shelf, and places it on the counter next to the stove. Next, he drops two pieces of toast into the toasting oven that his mother insists is the best choice for perfect toast.

By the time the toast is finished cooking, he has finished making his eggs. He looks around the large kitchen. A slight stirring down the hall reminds him the room will be busy soon. He decides to take his plate back to the loft.

Quiet time is never a bad idea.

When he settles into the bed again with his plate, his cuff alerts him of contact. Digging it out of his bag frustrates him until he sees who it is contacting him. He opens the projection, and settles it against the wall above his bed so he can eat. "Hey, what's up?"

Cerita's image shimmers against the wall. "Hi. It's the first time I'm using this from here. Had no clue how this would work, but hi." She is smiling and rushing someone away from where she's calling from. "How are you?"

After finishing his bite, he answers, "Good. I guess you've been up for a bit. Things seem busy there."

"I actually haven't slept yet." She shrugs. "I was going to do some training in the vampyre valley today. Would you be up for joining us?"

"Us?"

"Yeah. Darach, Journ, Calinda, and I."

"A reunion."

She nods. "Yeah. I guess it is." She bites on her lower lip briefly. "So, you joining us?"

He shrugs. "I've got nothing better going on today. Where and what time?"

"We're meeting at the mouth of the Tigre. Bring water gear. Calinda insists Mikayla can be convinced to join us, and she could teach us some water stuff. Meeting in about an hour, if you're up for it."

"I think training sounds exactly like what we need. Especially with my arm back at a hundred percent." He takes another bite.

"Great. See you there." Cerita's face is much happier than when she opened the connection.

The connection closes and he finishes breakfast. After cleaning his dishes and putting on his gear, he opens a portal to the mouth of the Tigre. He leaves a message for his parents and another of his master knight. He steps through the portal, and finds himself standing near Journ. His lips are taut, and brow is furrowed while he wipes down his blade.

James asks him, "Everything good?"

Journ nods silently.

James shrugs. "Everyone else here yet?"

Journ looks up, points toward the tree line, then returns his attention to the blade.

In the shadows are two people. One petite, the other nearly his height. When the taller pins the smaller's back to a tree, James looks away. It doesn't take him much to know what was going on and he wasn't ready to see her going forward in that way. He made a promise to himself that he would remain pleasant when needed, but honoring their people and traditions would remain most important.

Calinda appears with Mikayla a moment later. The wercat slinks up to James the moment she's out of the portal. "So, Elf, you ready for some water games?" Her eyebrows shoot up briefly, as she grins at him.

He sighs, rolls his eyes, and laughs. "You never give up do you?"

She purrs. "I do when I catch 'em."

"Oh, so that's how I get you off my back? Let you 'catch' me?"

Mikayla laughs. "Or that's how you get on your back. She's not so gentle."

James laughs, shakes his head, and begins securing his cuffs. When Calinda pinches his bottom he steps forward. "Too much."

The wercat pouts. "Awww . . . I thought it was just right." She winks and preps her gear.

After securing their collars and watching the knights prepare for water training, the guides settle in on the bank of the river together. She begins to stretch. "Mikayla isn't going easy on anyone. Cute or not. You'll wanna stretch."

He shrugs, and begins stretching. "Shouldn't we have our master knights somewhere nearby?"

"Why? You plan on drowning?"

He shakes his head. "Nope. Don't plan on letting anyone else do it either." His eyes shift toward the swiftly moving waters of the Tigre. There are few rocks as far as he can see, and although the river is moving rapidly, it's clear to the bottom through most of what they will encounter. "This isn't the worst of the rivers either."

"Nahhh, it's tame compared to the ones we swim in." Calinda switches positions. "On the real, you're not claimed or nothin' right?"

"Not claimed. Really, it wouldn't be right for me yet."

She shrugs. "Nah, I suppose not. But then there's a reason why Cats, Vamps, and Gobbies get along like we do."

"Each tribe has their own standards, both for health and other stuff." He switches positions and is caught off guard when Mikayla drops into the water. He watches her for a few moments, and smiles when she surfaces with a grin that spreads from ear to ear. "She always has this much fun?"

"We don't have much water back home, so yeah. The rivers we play in are toxic for her if she's in it too long. I haven't tried it that long so, I don't know." Calinda shrugs. "I'm glad she's relaxing here."

"I think I need to be spending more time in Atlantis." He watches the mer-woman jump and dive and surface again just to repeat the process.

"You think she's cute?"

James shakes his head. "I don't generally think like that, Calinda. I've got other things on my mind."

"Like your knight?"

James' features redden slightly while he explains, "Not like -" he's cut off by the sound of someone screaming in the trees. Faster than he can think, he's on his feet and sprinting toward the sound. Crossing into the shadows he finds Darach with a dagger through his arm, laughing. Cerita stands not far from him, trembling. "What happened?"

Calinda is right behind him, and Mikayla joins after.

Darach yanks the dagger from his arm, and looks at Cerita. "We were practicing how to throw the daggers. She missed her target, by a smidge."

"I didn't mean it. I'm so sorry." Cerita's hands shake as she takes the dagger from him.

Darach catches her with his free hand and pulls her in closer. "Watch. This is what your knowledge of your nanites can do for you." He rolls up the sleeve of his shirt to expose the cut on his arm. While they are yet watching, his nanites cover the wound and slowly pull his skin together. He flinches through parts, and soon, even that stops. Within moments, the wound stops bleeding entirely, and begins to heal. He smiles at her. "See, nothing to it."

Mikayla looks at the vampyre. "You sure you're okay? Don't need anything?"

Darach looks up at the mer-woman and nods. "It's just a little blood."

The trees start to move on their own. He feels his knees slacken. He curses under his breath, in an ancient language not heard on the surface in more millennium than can be easily counted. Using the tree he was just pinned to for support, he slides down it.

Mikayla is by his side. "Yeah, that's what I thought." She and Cerita steady him. "Cal, find him some food. He needs both kinds."

"I didn't lose that much blood, Mermaid." Darach blinks. The lighting around them seems to bend on the edges of his vision. "Okay, maybe I should have pulled the dagger faster."

Cerita shakes her head. "Well, showing off is what you do. Just don't let it kill you, okay?"

Mikayla rolls up her sleeve, but looks around while she does. "James, do you see any animals around?"

"A few birds higher up." He looks toward the tops of the trees.

"There were fish in the river too, but I doubt they'll be good for him. Can you get a bird down here?"

"Yep." James pulls out his crossbow, loads it, and sprints silently ahead.

Mikayla leans her arm toward Darach. "Here."

His eyes narrow and he shakes his head. "Not before I fuel the rest of me."

"You may not have that long." She scolds.

"Not true. The lightheadedness is already passing." He takes a deep breath, closes his eyes, and smirks. "Besides, human tastes better."

Cerita slaps him on the shoulder. "He'll be fine." When Mikayla looks at her quizzically, she responds, "No. No bite marks here."

"Good. That's not always a good sign between a vampyre and anyone." Mikayla stares at him hard but speaks with a warning tone. "Especially one with certain unique habits."

"Glare all you want, Mikayla. It does nothing for you." Darach keeps his eyes closed. "Now, I think you will need a targeting enhancement for your dagger, my beautiful human."

"Not your human." Cerita rests on her butt. "And maybe."

Mikayla asks, "Where were you aiming?"

"The branch above him."

Mikayla's eyes follow the length of the tree upward. When she realizes that even with Darach's arm fully extended, the tree branch was still a long way from him she drops her eyes back to Cerita. "Ah, yeah. Targeting upgrade. Lot's more practice needed. Hand the dagger to Journ." She nods her head as their silent wolf friend approaches with a small deer. "Oh. Perfect!"

Mikayla hops up, takes the deer from Journ and does a quick assessment. Making certain it's full grown, albeit small, she swings the dagger out of her hip and plunges it into the neck of the animal. As the blood begins to pour out, she drags the animal to Darach before it begins to coagulate.

Darach sinks his teeth deep into the animal until it no longer struggles. When he is unable to derive another bit of the precious liquid from the animal, he pulls his mouth from the carcass. "I suppose this is a mixed tribe survival game now."

Cerita turns back toward her friend to find blood still soaking into his skin. Her stomach churns. "Seems like that." She stands, and slides out into the open.

"First time she's seen you feed, I take it?" Mikayla gestures toward the human.

"Yes. It's not something that should have been needed, but accidents happen." Darach looks up as James returns with the bird, also struggling to break free. He meets the elf and quickly drains the bird of blood as well.

Once he's finished, he rejoins the group, holding the bird. "Well, these would make meals, once cooked."

Journ nods in acknowledgment while he is preparing the deer.

James makes quick work of cleaning the bird.

Mikayla suggests, "How about we leave Darach, Calinda, and Journ here to finish cooking while you, and Cerita join me in the river for some training?"

"That wouldn't be bad. We could switch in a bit." James hands the bird to Calinda, who made it back with a small bird of her own. "I know you'll find something to do with it."

She shrugs. "I'm sure I'll find someone to do too, while you're away." She winks at the elf again. "Can't be getting bored or anything."

Everyone laughs, and James responds, "No, of course not."

The friends split up. With Calinda, Journ, and Darach working on food preparation, James and Cerita are able to get an extensive water lesson from Mikayla. It's a lesson both are grateful to have. They return to the group with fish to add to the meal, and Mikayla takes Journ and Darach out to the river.

Calinda drags Cerita off to the wild grasses. Together they gather greens that can be eaten with the rest of their meal. Calinda makes a point to not only help Cerita identify which grasses can be eaten, but also which ones taste good when they are. She also gives her a primer of information about how each grass will affect the different tribes. By the time they return to the campsite, James has the fire warm and is cooking some of the fish.

By evening, water training is done and everyone is warming themselves by the fire. As a group they talk of friends, and new training ideas. They share campfire secrets, and end the day relaxed and happy. Cerita stretches out on the grass by the fire. This moment reminds her that even with all of the changes around her, nothing could be more peaceful than sleeping next to a warm fire. The last thing she recalls is a long coat being draped over her by Journ.

Chapter 2

Journ sits in front of the fire as the last of the embers burn out. He stirs the remnants of their wood fueled flames. A wind blows, and he can smell a change. His eyes fixate on Calinda, who stirs. His lips go taut. His cuff alerts him of a data message that he accepts. After reading it, he moves into the woods to gather dry, dead wood that has fallen from the trees. Another message comes in before he is out of the tree line. He grunts while reading over it. By the time he arrives at the campsite, Calinda is sitting up trying to warm herself by the nearly cold pit. He places the firewood within the pit, and restarts the fire.

Her arms wrap around her shoulders. "You're up early."

He nods. "You need medical."

She scowls. "No. I'm fine."

He shakes his head, points to his nose, and then returns his attention to bringing the fire to a level that will warm everyone as well as cook breakfast.

She turns away from him. "Don't discuss it."

He sighs.

As everyone begins to stir, he gathers his belongings.

Cerita sits next to the fire as he begins to fill his leather bag. "You're leaving early?"

"Duty." Journ responds while sealing his bag.

"You seem to have more to do than we do." James settles in next to him with some fruit he's acquired. "Everything okay?"

He nods.

"You have enough supplies?" Cerita reaches into her bag as she's talking.

"Yep."

"Oh, okay." She lowers her eyes, "Well, you know how to reach me when you've got time."

He nods. Moments later, he strolls toward the river, activates a portal, and disappears.

Calinda crawls over to James and nibbles off the fruit in his hand. "Yum. I bet you'd be sweet after eating that." She purrs.

He hangs his head. "You're ..."

"Too much to handle?" Mikayla offers an end for his sentence. "Down, girl. He's not for nibbling on."

Calinda mock pouts at Mikayla, and the two laugh.

Cerita smiles. "You know, James, I don't think she's going to let up on any of that."

"Nope. I have a distinct feeling we'll be fifty years into our jobs and still listening to her overtly flirtatious behaviors." He looks over at Cerita, meeting her eyes steadily for the first time in a long while. "Think we'll be able to stand her that long?"

Cerita laughs. "She's a good friend and guide. Eh, maybe."

Mikayla laughs. "Yeah, she's good in a fight too. I just think she would prefer to keep her pretty little paws clean."

Calinda sits up, looks at everyone, and says, "It's not my fault I have no problems with my sexuality." She pauses briefly and smirks. "Or anyone else's either."

Darach pulls his hood well over his head. "Seems I'm going home early too. I just got called back for training with the master knight."

"Everything good?" Cerita slides next to him, and peers under his hood.

He lowers his voice and whispers to the human, "I'm told it is. Something is off though." His hand wraps around hers and squeezes it tight for a brief moment. He raises his voice when he continues, "It's always good back home. It's near silence with all the peace going on." He chuckles. His eyes meet James and Cerita and briefly it occurs to him that neither have seen anything he has. "Silence is good."

Mikayla looks down at her communication cuff. "Cal, we've got an assignment." She looks up. "Guess one day and night is enough for now. Get your gear. We're heading to the mainland."

All three of the remaining turn to look at her. James speaks what everyone is thinking, "You're coming to the mainland? Earth?"

"Yes. We're to be briefed."

It takes everyone a few minutes to put out the fire and collect their things. As they finish, Cerita receives the same message Mikayla has. Her stomach trembles. She forwards a message to her parents and calms herself. "I need to dig up my sword."

Darach extends his hand. "Come. I've got to get mine too."

They walk together into the trees and return a bit dirtier, both with their swords slung over their backs. He leans over, brushes his lips against hers again, without response.

He shakes his head and laughs. In a whisper he asks, "So, not getting that kiss, hu?"

"I said we would have to give it some thought." She pokes him in the ribs.

He laughs. "Fine. I've never had a human woman so stubborn."

She grins. "That's because you hadn't met me."

Mikayla calls her. "Cerita, we need to go."

She nods. "We do. Talk to you soon, right?"

"Without doubt." Darach turns, opens his portal, and steps through.

Cerita grabs her smaller bag, and waits with James for Mikayla to open a portal to her father. The four step through and into the training facility. The lights are low. In the main room, they see the usual training layout. It seems the apprentices appear to have arrived first, but something feels off.

Calinda stands taller, with her claws extended. "Regardless of what our eyes show us, we are not alone."

James activates his lightweight armor. His bow is attached at the lower part of his arm, and he loads it faster than is seen.

Cerita and Mikayla withdraw their swords. Within seconds, both knights are equally prepared.

"Footsteps." The young women look to James, who adds, "Out back." He gestures toward the back door.

They remain silent for several more moments before the rear door swings open.

Before they enter the room, the unmistakable sound of metal on concrete is heard as two master knights and a master guide enter the rear of the building. Mikayla starts to withdraw her sword, but Calinda shakes her head. Her ears flicker and her eyes look toward the window.

James silently steps forward toward the mat. He lifts his arm and levels it with a curtain that covers the large window near the front door. As the door in the rear opens into the training room, bright light floods the room enough to see a shadow. He lets loose the bolt and strikes his target.

A loud cry carries across the room.

The knights and their apprentices draw their swords.

Master Frederickson commands, "Step out."

A slender woman steps from behind the drapes. Her straggly, black hair hangs below her shoulders. Her hand holds where the bolt is lodged in her upper arm. Deep red blood trails down on either side of her arm.

"Who are you?" Ralph asks, sheathing his sword, but not withdrawing his armor.

"Kendra." Her voice shakes and she drops to her knees. Tears stream down her face.

"Why are you here?" Sacha steps forward toward the girl, and kneels Her eyes narrow as she focuses the depth of the wound in the young woman's arm. "It's not bad." She gestures toward Calinda. "Take care of that."

Calinda and James put their weapons away, and move to the young woman's side to begin working on the wound.

The bewildered girl stumbles her first attempts at explaining herself, but eventually gets out, "I didn't believe them. They said you were real, but . . ."

Calinda focuses her nanites to conceal her feline likeness. "Who said we were real?"

"They call themselves protectors of humans, or hunters of . . . " She looks away from Calinda. "you"

Ralph groans. "Hunters. He's recruiting."

Mikalya asks, "Who's recruiting?"

"Your assignments. We'll give you more in a moment." Ralph returns his attention to the girl to ask, "Kendra, do you know who you're talking to?"

"He said you are knights and people who want to take over. Vampyres who'll eat us. Others." She drops her yes as Calinda places a final bandage on her arm. She softly mutters, "Thanks."

"How did you get in?" James asks.

"The lock was picked." Kendra looks away.

Before the girl finishes, Chandra stands at the door with a finger extended toward the lock. She is intently focused on watching it for several moments before turning back to Ralph. Her nanite enhanced felnoid eyes identify some scratches through the small hole in the locking mechanism. "You need a tumbler upgrade. It's been stripped."

He acknowledges Chandra with a nod but focuses on Kendra. "I should have you arrested."

The girl's eyes grow wide. "But . . . but you shot me. You can't."

"I can. You broke into my business. My trainee was simply defending us." Ralph withdraws his armor and folds his arms over his chest. Even as an aged human, he's still intimidating.

The girl looks up. "No. Please."

His angry, even tone remains intensely focused on the intruding girl. "What do you think we should do right now?"

"I . . . I can tell you where we're meeting? Or I can forget I met you. Or . . ." Tears begin to fall down her face again. "Just please don't hurt me."

"Master, may I speak with her?" Cerita steps forward, and when Ralph gestures, she kneels within arm's reach of the girl. "It's all kinda surprising isn't it?"

She nods, tears stream down her cheeks faster.

"Being human has left us thinking we're the only ones." She reaches out and takes the girl's hand. "Do you know everyone here is of Earth? Did he tell you that?"

The girl shakes her head while sobbing.

"It's true. Everyone in this room can be traced to the same place. It's kinda amazing that way. You heard about the cave men?" When the girl nods again, Cerita continues, "There were others too, did you know that?" This time the girl shakes her head.

"Yeah. The scientists have proven many different types of DNA sprang up in the same area. My friends are just examples of that. We aren't here to harm anyone though."

"Why?"

"Why are we here?" She nods, and Cerita answers, "We want to live, like everyone else. We want to be with our families and those we love. You have family right?"

Kendra sniffles, "No."

"What happened?"

"They were killed. Their blood was drained, like beasts." She sobs even harder. Her body shudders with each breath.

James immediately responds, "It wasn't a vampyre."

The girl looks up at him from her crouched state. "How would you know?"

"Because there haven't been vampyres living here in a few centuries, and the last to visit came for their last rites a few months ago. There are none." He stands not far from the girls, watchful.

Kendra looks at the elf. "Why should I believe you?"

Cerita reassures her, "It's our job to know. We are here to protect those who need our protection. Sometimes it's humanity, but usually, it's from people like Jacob Hines. People who don't understand."

James mutters, "Or worse, people who hunt and kill our tribes anyway."

The girl cowers away from James.

Cerita shakes her head. "He's not a vampyre."

"Prove it." Kendra glares at him through her tears.

He sighs, throws open the curtain and exposes himself to sunlight. "Not. A. Vampyre."

She nods. "Who killed them then?"

"We don't know, but I promise we'll find out." Cerita turns to Ralph, who nods. "Kendra, we will need the information you can provide us with. Okay?"

She shakes her head. "No. He said he'd find the killers and he will avenge my parents."

Cerita hangs her head.

Calinda looks at her mother, then Sacha. Both give her an even stare. "What should we do?"

Ralph says, "Let her go. If she tries to go to the police about this, she's the one who will be charged with breaking and entering. I have a permit for every weapon in this building and a license recognizing their use."

Mikalya flatly adds, "No one outside of the hunters will believe her claims anyway."

Cerita lifts her face to the young woman's again. "Hey, I know this is confusing, and I know you're hurting a lot right now, but we really do want to help. It's what we do."

Kendra looks at Cerita for a few minutes, then her eyes drift from one to the other of those in the room. "Brier Woods. There is a very large cabin, and a few trailers out there. Jacob's family owns it. We go out there a few weekends a month. He brings some people from his hunters place, thingy too. They teach us stuff so we know how to stop . . ." Her voice trembles as she struggles to continue.

"Shh . . ." Cerita wraps an arm over the girl's shoulders. "We'll find out who took them from you. If it turns out to be one of ours, we'll make sure they never hurt anyone else again. If it happens they are not, we'll still stop them. I promise."

Kendra nods, forces herself to her feet, and walks out the door. No one stops her. No one tries to slow her down. Chandra even opens the door for her. The moment the Atlanteans are alone, all the armor withdraws. Weapons are returned to their holders.

Chandra asks, "You placed the tracker?"

Calinda nods. "Yep."

Ralph looks at James. "Good. You both did well."

Cerita looks at her master knight. "What do we do now?"

"Now, we determine who is trying to fake a vampyre killing." Ralph rolls his neck.

"But why would they have planted her here?" Mikayla walks to her father as he moves to the computer desk.

"To make sure we know what's going on. It's more likely to draw us into this if we are also doing the research." James closes his eyes. "You did good, Cerita."

Sacha nods. "You did. I'm not sure most of us could have been as compassionate."

"Just made sense to me." She looks to the corner where everyone seems to be gathering. "Did you find something?"

Ralph nods. "Kendra Ranee Crane is the only surviving daughter of Richard and Stacey Crane, found dead in their home three days ago. Cause of death is listed as unnatural. And according to the report, they were found in their bed, coated in blood, but none was in their body. That's not typical for any vampyre we're aware of. There's no mess left behind, even from the predators of the past." His eyes shift from the screen to Cerita on the ground. "Her parents were the owners of the butcher shop down the road from James' family farm."

James groans inwardly. "I never met her before, but I've been with my parents when we've had to drop off a steer or cow." He lowers his head. "They were good people."

"Well, it looks like Kendra was quite the handful. She's got an arrest record pages long." Ralph scrolls through a list of petty thefts, drug offenses, and assorted other misdemeanor charges. "She's no killer though."

Cerita tilts her head and peers at her teacher. "You can see all of that?"

James reminds her, "Freedom of Information Act."

"Oh, right."

"And yes, to answer your concerns, most of us can hack sapien security computers, if need be." Ralph stands from his chair. "Remember that Atlantis had computer systems by the time the city was sank. That was many millennia before we were a thought in our parents' minds."

Sacha sighs loudly. "So, we have a girl who's seen a portal open loose on the streets of a relatively small town. She's a grieving junkie who now believes a vampyre killed her parents. She's associated with a fringe group of the local human hunters, and she knows exactly how many Atlanteans are here, thanks to her fringe group leader. This is not going to be a fun assignment."

Chapter 3

Cerita and James settle in the trees near the large cabin in Brier Woods. They followed Kendra's signal there right after school let out, and now as the sun sets, they are watching a crowd gathering. "Just information tonight."

He nods. "Just information. From what I'm seeing though, we need to change your training."

"Why?"

"These people aren't well trained, but there are a lot of them." His feet hang from a strong branch. From here, they are able to see much of the camp, including a new fire being built in the center of it all. "You can't beat me yet, let alone that many."

"I can hold my own just fine, thank you." She shifts so she's closer to the trunk of the tree. Her bag is hanging on a branch just above them. "Need to put out the recorders."

He nods, stuffs his hand in his pocket, and withdraws a small, flat, round, golden colored device. He runs his thumb over the top, and it expands into a larger ball.

The sound of the device form changing is minimal, so when she activates hers as well, he has to look over to check.

Both gently toss the golden balls in the direction of the crowd. Then they use their communication cuffs to command the movement of their recording devices, as well as to receive the data streamed back from them.

The recording balls go in different directions, always moving, recording, and sending information. The vast amount of information being transmitted keeps them both transfixed on their cuffs for another hour before she breaks the silence. "Crap."

He jerks his head toward her. "What?"

"Problem."

He slides next to her so he can look at her transmission. With his head nearly on her shoulder, he's able to identify Jacob Hines and two of the other hunters. Between his buddies is a single woman with flame red hair and a steely look he's familiar with. "They are in trouble."

"What makes you say that? She doesn't look like she's there of her own free will."

"Nope. More than that, she looks pissed. She's not cowering, even after he's struck her. She's not responding to much." James shifts to look at Cerita. "That's not good for someone who's looking for a response. The first moment he lets his guard down with this one, she'll take advantage somehow."

Cerita looks at him briefly, then returns her focus to the woman. "How dare he hit her like he has, but now to take a weapon . . .? James, there's no way she's going to get through -"

The woman moves with the speed needed to avoid an oncoming bullet only feet away.

"She avoided it?"

"Yes. You can still see?"

"Nope. I can see your expression. She's one of ours." He gazes at his readings, as his device sends back data from around the bonfire outside of the building Cerita's is in.

"But what is she?"

He shrugs. "She's tall enough. Could be an elf. Fast enough too."

"Her hands are bound." She informs him without taking her eyes off the video being sent to her.

"And I didn't see her struggling."

"True." Cerita settles her recording device in a house plant in the same room. "I'll keep an eye on things here."

"Might be a good idea to listen in too. I know we said we'd do that later, but given the situation, might be a good idea." He continues to move his recording device through the growing crowd around the fire. When his device happens upon Kendra stretched between two men, he shakes his head and grumbles, "Human morality, or lack thereof."

"You want to say that again?" Cerita looks over at him.

"Nope." He chuckles, then he looks up at the movements in front of them. "Seems they're going to sit around and dog our people all night." He looks over at Cerita. "It's getting late. Try to get comfortable, and I'll watch for now. I don't require as much sleep as you do."

She nods, leans on the trunk of the tree, and attempts to sleep. It takes her a while, but she finally drifts off. Her device continues to record the actions in the room around the plant she stored it in. Although the sound of the room continues to play in her ear, it is the sounds of the crowd near the fire that wakes her from the nap. Groggy, she stretches, yawns, and asks, "What's going on?"

"Not sure. Kendra got really interested in something Hines was saying." They both focus their attention on the activities below.

She lowers her device voice replay. Together, the Atlanteans listen to his recording device on low.

Hines is standing near the fire. He pours a beer onto the flame, making it shoot up briefly. Everyone around him laughs. "Okay. Okay. Everyone quiet for a moment." He pauses, but the group only starts to quiet before he continues with, "I promised you confirmation, and you will have it."

The crowd gets loud again. Cheers are heard over anything he is trying to say. It takes several minutes before the recorder can pick up his voice alone again.

Hines tells his crowd of wanna-be hunters, "We have caught one of those vile creatures. One who could have killed this beautiful woman's family." He pulls Kendra to her feet and wraps an arm around her waist. "Tonight, we avenge her!"

The crowd roars loudly again. It seems as though everyone in the crowd is cheering the idea of avenging the 'creature'.

There is a shuffle near Cerita's recording device. She checks on it to find three men dragging the redheaded woman out of the cabin, and into the crowd. She is shoved through the bodies reaching for, grabbing at, and doing what they can to offend her.

Cerita's eyes divert to the display below as the woman is brought before the fire. She can feel the adrenaline rise. All sense of sleepiness is gone. She begins assessing the situation for the best approach.

Cerita whispers to James, "I'm sending Master Knight Frederickson our info, and getting suited up."

He nods. "So much for info only."

Cerita doesn't take her eyes off the scene around the fire for long. Each time she looks up, they are pushing the woman's lips up to show her sharper eye teeth.

They aren't extended though. The only reason Cerita is certain they aren't exposed from this distance is because the woman would need to feed, and that much would be more obvious than simply extended teeth.

By the time Cerita's done with her message, and all of her supplies are in her bag, she hears the tone shift. Looking at James, she asks, "What's going on?"

"He's talking about burning her at and with sunrise."

"How long until?" Cerita's eyes begin to scan the horizon, looking for east. As he confirms her fears she notices the first rays of light pierce the sky. She drops her head. "We don't have much time."

"Nope. Set the device to transmit all data to Atlantis, then to explode."

"I can do that?" She starts to review the controls on her connection to the recording device and nods. "Found it."

"Good." The elf is on his feet, and then on the ground in seconds. "I set mine for five minutes, and to autopilot into the fire. That should keep them all busy for a while."

Cerita mentions, "You know she could be a day walker and have no problems, right?"

"I know." He reaches up and helps his knight to the ground. "But that's not the majority of vampyre kind."

"Yeah. I can still hope." Cerita half laughs, draws her sword, and extends her helmet. "Down the center to the woman, and then into the woods together. We'll port the first chance we can get away."

He nods, loads his crossbow, and sets up a second on his other arm.

They make their way to the encampment of drunken men and women waiting to watch a vampyress burn. The rowdy group hardly notices the pair entering until they push more than halfway through the crowd. At the point they are acknowledged, one man grabs Cerita by the arm, only to find himself forcefully removed from his seat. As she drops the man back down on the dirt path, she levels her sword briefly at him. With a look of anger, she withdraws it. He scrambles back to the end of the group.

James lifts both arms and levels them with the on-comers. The handful of actual hunters in the group reach for their weapons of choice. Two of them level themselves with the knight and her guide. Hines begins to make an even greater display.

"See! These fools come for their brethren." His words slur while he speaks. He laughs, lifts a handgun, and aims it for Cerita. "Don't come any further, Knight. I know your armor isn't going to deflect a bullet."

"You don't know what you're doing, Hines. You're asking for trouble you can't handle." Cerita brings her sword to striking level. "Don't put these people in harm's way for your own inadequacies."

Someone throws a beer at the intruders.

James presses forward again, even as the two other hunters refocus their weapons on him. "You're going to want to be away from that fire in another minute or two." His eyes lock with the vampryess' briefly, and she acknowledges him with a nod.

James lets lose both bolts, striking the weapons out of the hands of the hunters trying to stop him.

Cerita steps forward and slices through the bindings on the woman, who immediately slides both hands under the back of her shirt and pulls out a pair of sai. Cerita laughs, shakes her head, and turns her focus to Hines. "You're going to tell this rowdy crowd to back away from the fire."

An explosion rattles the ground as windows in the back of the cabin blow out. The crowd begins to scramble, and the sun rises on the chaos.

The vampyress looks at the sky, and then at the crowd trying to burn her. Her teeth descend to visible over her lower lip. She grins.

Cerita looks at her and gestures to the forest. Without another word, the three move, fighting anyone who attempts to stop them along the way.

When they are about to break free of the chaos, the explosion in the fire sends every person running in all directions.

To get control of the crowd again, Hines shoots his gun straight in the air.

James, Cerita, and the vampyre take the moment to escape into the deeper woods area. Once they are far enough away, Cerita opens a portal. "You're safe. We'll get you food."

The woman looks at the bright light as it shifts into a stable portal. "What is that?"

James retracts his faceplate. "It's a stable wormhole between here and a safe location. They are waiting on us. How have you never seen one before?"

"I'll walk." She spins the sai in her hand and tucks them back into a holder on her lower back.

"What? Where are you going?" Cerita withdraws her armor.

"Anywhere away from those freaks." The woman begins to walk away, deeper into the woods. "I'll see you around, Atlanteans."

Cerita and James exchange looks and close the portal. Once they catch up they ask, "What is your name?"

"I'm Tasha. I am forsaken." She stops and looks at the pair.

"Forsaken?"

"I'm sure you know what the word means." Her eyes lock with James. "You're not human, are you?"

"No. I'm not." He tilts his head. "Don't you still need to feed?"

She looks down at the cuts on her arms. All are already healing. "I'll feed later." She gestures to the rays of light piercing the trees. "If you don't mind, I'd like to find a nice comfortable, dark place for the day."

"We can help with that." Cerita lifts her sword. "The portals work like gateways. We can get you someplace dark, fast."

She shakes her head. "Nah. I'm not for all that science fiction stuff. I'd rather use my legs. They've served me well for centuries."

"Fine." Cerita rummages through her bag, and hands her a small business card. "Meet us here tonight. It's in town. We'll make sure to be there around midnight, so you have travel time."

Tasha accepts the business card, and looks at it carefully. "Fredrickson Training Hall?"

"Just trust us, please. We'll make sure we have ample for you to feed on, physical and otherwise."

"Well, I guess it's best to get the address I've been searching for from the source." She tilts her head and looks at the young pair. They display exactly what she has feared.

"You know nothing of the Forsaken. Alright. I'll meet you there." The vampyress spins and walks away.

The knight and her guide enter the portal to the training facility and step into the building.

** *** **

By nightfall, the exhausted elf arrives back to the facility to find it dimly lit. He hauls a small tote full of food through the front door. Stepping in, he finds the master knights in full armor, except helmets. "What's wrong?"

"The local head of the hunters is on his way here. He said Hines is leading trouble this way." Sacha looks over Ralph's shoulder. "And it looks like the council would like us to contain it without injuries."

Ralph adds, "And they want your Forsaken brought to Atlantis."

"We didn't tell her we'd force her there. It was about getting to know her, and what she meant. I thought all of the Forsaken died years ago." James unpacks some of the food with Calinda's help.

"It appears that isn't what happened." Mikayla adds, "She's here, and she shouldn't be."

"She didn't know what a portal was. That's so odd. I thought all vampyre would know and use them." Cerita contributes as she enters the building. "I just hope she comes."

"Forsaken are different. They aren't of Atlantis. Could have been, but didn't make it to the island before the sinking." Calinda stands near James in the center of the room.

A moment later, someone knocks at the door.

Cerita grins. She opens the door and finds a squad of hunters at the door. She swallows.

Her smile fades fast. She announces, "Master Knight, I believe this is for you."

Ralph greets the lead hunter, Edward Jones. "Welcome, Edward. Come in." He pulls the door open wide and the hunters enter the large room. Everyone begins to eye each other suspiciously.

Cerita extends her hand to the lead hunter. "Hello, Mr. Jones. I'm Cerita Guzman. I think I might go to school with your daughter."

Her warm smile and welcome is returned. "Cerita, hu? Kassandra hasn't mentioned you, but it's possible. She doesn't talk much to me about school."

She nods. "Kassandra 'Kassy' Jones. She's in basketball, right?"

He nods, releasing her hand. "Yes. It's good to meet you."

"Nice to meet you too."

He gestures to the others with him. "Ron, Jeff, Jared, and Phil, this is Cerita, and Ralph, and their friends."

Each one in turn shakes hands with the knight and his apprentice.

Ralph then extends an arm to the others in the room. "This is Knight Sacha Rines, our daughter and her apprentice Mikayla, and her guide, Chandra." The ladies acknowledge the hunters. "Chandra's daughter is Calinda, who is Mikayla's Guide in Apprentice."

Calinda smiles and allows a purr to come out even though she's using her nanites to conceal her feline attributes.

James stands and crosses to the hunters. "I'm Cerita's Guide in Apprentice." He shakes hands with each of the hunters and then tucks his hair behind his pointed ears.

Ralph gives James a look before speaking to Edward again. "Thank you for the help."

"Of course. We all want the same thing in this one. No blood shed, and no chaos. It does no one any good to have attention drawn to what we do." Edward nods at Jeff. "Watch the window while we determine what steps we're going to take."

Without a word, the tall, dark skinned man pulls his long brown trench coat over his shoulders a little tighter while walking to the window. He slips his hand across his middle and into a pocket on the inside of the coat.

Edward, Ralph, and Sacha settle behind a computer and begin to discuss the situation. The other hunters mingle until there is another knock at the door. This time, Jeff waves someone over. "Looks like a human woman," he mutters.

James strolls over and opens it to Tasha. "Come in."

She steps in, leery of the crowd. "Is the party on my account?" She allows her teeth to become visible.

James explains, "No. The jerks from last night seem to be planning to pay us a visit." He yanks his thumb back toward the men in long brown trench coats. "Those are hunters who will stand with us to stop them."

"Good. You'll need all the help you can get. Those people are unhinged." Her voice remains even. "You spoke of food, and I assume you expect to interrogate me."

James gets her a chair, and pours a large glass of a deep red liquid. "Yes. Here. Replenish first."

Cerita explains, "I doubt it'll be an interrogation."

Cerita and Mikayla settle down with seats of their own while Calinda sits on the mats nearby with the food spread out. Calinda begins to prepare plates and passes them out to everyone, while Tasha drinks.

"This is fresh?" She looks at the elf.

"I drained it just a short while ago." James settles on a mat and starts to devour a sandwich.

"Sheep?"

"Goat, actually. It's closer to the most ideal blood type. Our sheep are out west right now." He responds between bites.

"It's good. Thank you." She finishes the first and a second glass full, and is finally able to bite into food on the plate before her.

"What brought you here, Tasha?"

She smirks. "You invited me."

Cerita laughs. "Right, but what brought you to this area?"

"I was looking for you, actually. I had heard that Earth's Knight might be here, and so I came." She pauses long enough to take a small bite before asking, "Safe to assume that's not you?"

Cerita nods. "Not yet, anyway." She looks over at the three at the computer. "The two not in brown trench coats are knights. He is Earth's Knight. I am his apprentice, for now."

Mikayla nods. "Calinda and I are from Teratura. It's a planet for Atlanteans."

Tasha nods while eating. "I guess I'll need to speak with him, but something tells me now isn't the time."

She looks away from the meeting between the knights and hunter. "You said the thugs from last night are coming?" She finishes off her sandwich and starts in on the fruit.

"Yep." Mikayla leans back. "We don't know what they have planned, but we need to be ready. The hunters are the ones who told us to expect problems, and offered to help."

"Why would they do that?" Her voice is flat.

"Because they don't want a war with Atlantis. Their goal is to keep our people in check, in their minds. They say it's not to massacre us." Calinda sips her juice.

"You sound like you believe that as much as I do." Tasha looks at the wercat directly.

"We didn't establish other planets without reason." Cynicism is evident in Calinda's tone.

Tasha chuckles. "That concept is hard to grasp."

"We have help now, and no idea what's coming, or where." Cerita finishes a sip of her juice. "That's what matters right now."

"Yeah." Calinda looks at her human-esque hands. "Right." Her eyes lift to the human girl. "But you're not the one hiding in your own skin."

Tasha interrupts the conversation. "Well, if the forsaken have their way, none of this will matter. People like the mob from yesterday will have good reason to behave that way." Tasha looks from apprentice to apprentice. "I suspect you'll be very busy."

Calinda sits up quickly. Her eyes focus on James. "Do you smell that?" Her nose twitches.

"Smell what?" Then his eyes widen. "Gasoline. Master Knight! Do you smell that?"

Ralph, Edward, and Sacha are already on their feet searching the room. Jeff indicates that he has yet to see anyone, but now he can smell it too. Then he looks down. "Move! Get out!" the hunter calls loudly.

Not a second later, the outer wall bursts into flames, and the ceiling starts to drip liquid into the large room. James extends his arm to open a portal, but Tasha stops him. "You sure that won't make this whole place explode?"

Ralph opens one near him, closer to the wall that's crumbled. "We'll be fine. Everyone through."

Tasha shakes her head as everyone, even the hunters, tumble through the purple and black spiraling hole. Sacha grabs the vampyress by the arm and forces her through.

Everyone tumbles onto a soft brown carpet in a small room that fills quickly. There are no windows, but the artificial lighting illuminates the room completely. When the last of the Atleanteans and their company tumble out of the portal, a few bricks follow as the portal closes.

Ralph hangs his head. "Great."

Edward looks at him. "I'm sorry. I had no idea he would . . . I'm sorry, man."

Calinda reverts to her natural state, and her mother places two hands on her shoulder. "Don't move, Calinda."

The hunters step back from her as far as the room allows.

Edward looks at the girl. He starts to speak, but James cuts him off.

"Calinda, every one of them would have died in there with us. Don't stress 'em." James looks to Edward, and then his hunters.

Jeff turns to James. "I'm just glad you guys had the way out."

Sacha leans against the wall. "You do know the council's going to have your head, right?"

Ralph responds. "It was the first place I thought of. It's far enough away that we are all safe. They'd rather not lose good people over changeable laws."

"Laws?" the hunter introduced as Jared seems to grasp where they are. "We're *there*?"

"'There' where?" Ron asks.

"Atlantis." Edward's tone is shocked.

Tasha groans.

Sacha looks at the woman. "Not where you want to be?"

"Under millions of gallons of water and fish? Nope." The redheaded woman begins pacing along an inner wall. "Why are we in such a small room?"

"This is where knights stay, specifically, where I stay, when I'm here. Barracks." Ralph folds his arms across his chest.

"Take me back to land. This . . . this isn't going to work." She continues to pace, now pulling her sai out and flipping them every so often. "I can't do this."

Sacha looks to Ralph and Chandra. "There's not enough room to safely open the portal in here. We'll need to step out and check a few things before we know if it's safe to do in the hallway. Wait here."

The mer-woman pushes off the wall, grabs her best friend, and Calinda, and walks through a door that blends in with the wall.

Ralph mutters, "So many reasons that woman . . ." He laughs to himself.

Mikayla responds to him. "Mom feels the same way." She laughs.

Cerita looks at the pair, and then to everyone else in the room. "James, remind me to ask you about the laws we haven't gone over yet."

"Of course."

A few minutes later, Sacha returns. "We're safe. Chandra is taking Calinda for a walk. She still needs to cool down. Ralph, do you want to do the honors? I'm thinking across the street from your building, or what's left of it."

"No. By now, the authorities are working to put the fire out." Ralph steps out the door and Sacha encourages everyone to follow him into the darkened hallway.

"We'll go through to a park down the street. If anything comes of it, we'll simply claim it was a training exercise, outside the facility." He turns to Tasha. "You may want to put those away again."

Tasha nods, spins the sai one more time, then tucks them back into place.

The bright light flashes, the vortex adjusts, and the portal solidifies. Cerita steps through first. Mikayla follows with James close behind. Ralph encourages Tasha, who ultimately steps through. The hunters follow, and Sacha steps in with Ralph. Finding themselves in the lush park full of fields, trees, and various soccer or baseball layouts, they take a moment to breathe.

Sacha turns to Ralph, "You ready to see what happened?"

"It was just a place. Probably time to move on again anyway." He leads the walk back to where his training facility used to be. As he arrives, there are police cars, fire trucks, and a plethora of other emergency vehicles scouring the street. The fire is nearly out, and the moment he is visible, a man in a dark leather jacket approaches him.

"You're Ralph Frederickson?" He stands shorter than Ralph, and has far more gray on his head than most.

"Yep. What happened to my place?" Ralph scowls.

"We've been trying to reach you for fifteen minutes. Seems a gas line broke and blew up your building." He gestures toward the mess ahead of him. "It's about out now. I just need you to answer a few questions for me."

"Of course. Let me speak with my students first, and I've got quite a few questions of my own."

"Students?" The man looks over at the larger crowd. "Didn't expect you'd have so many so late at night."

"It's a testing night. However, we didn't expect a few minutes outside of the building for more trying exercise would mean returning to no building." Ralph extends his arm to the disarray.

"I can understand that. It seems you had good timing though. I'd hate to see what would have happened if you tested inside tonight." The older man pauses briefly before pulling a pen out.

"I'll be over talking to the fire chief. If you don't see me, ask for Detective O'Connor." After scribbling on a piece of paper, he hands it to Ralph. "See ya in a few." Then he walks away.

Ralph opens the folded paper and tenses. "I think everyone who doesn't have to play the part of the injured owner should go home." He looks up at Edward. "We'll talk tomorrow."

"You sure?"

"Yes. I need to deal with this, and you have something else to deal with." Ralph gestures to the corner where three men are standing.

Edward looks over his shoulder and nods. "Yep. Something else to deal with. We'll catch up over coffee."

The hunters stalk past the Atlanteans toward the small gathering of men that appear to be watching what's going on. Edward's hand is settled under his long trench coat.

Cerita looks at the aftermath. "I don't think either one of us are getting our cars."

James gestures to a burnt, crumpled vehicle in front of what used to be the facility. "I don't think I want that now."

Cerita sees her car on the other side of the road from the demolished building. "Mine's a mess." She sighs. "I'll check on it tomorrow."

Mikayla shakes her head. "So much destruction."

Tasha silently walks away from it all.

"Mikayla, how about you find a way home with Cerita tonight, and I'll touch base with you in the morning too? It'll give me time to help your dad with this mess." Sacha looks at Ralph who nods in agreement.

She shrugs and looks at Cerita. "You cool?"

"Yep. Cool."

"Okay. Then the three of us are heading back to the park. I'm not walking from here." James gestures for them to get moving.

Sacha and Ralph make their way to the detective.

The detective walks with them to a nearby late-night restaurant. Once the three of them order drinks, Detective O'Connor scribbles a few things on a paper and passes them over to Ralph. "We both know what we need to know. I need to know where to find this person, though."

Ralph opens the page and finds Jacob Hines' name written down. "Why?"

O'Connor looks at Ralph, then Sacha, and back to Ralph. "You want me to spell this one out for you?"

Sacha nods. "It would be helpful. Yes."

The man's eyes dart around the room and he lowers his tone to a whisper. "Some people are unhappy with what he's doing. Some people are aware of his vendetta against those he can't explain. That's on him. Some have seen enough, scientifically and otherwise, to prove what the facts are. This loose gun needs stopped."

Ralph leans forward before he responds. "You know enough to know what was going on in my training hall, you know enough to be assured we'll handle our business."

"Good. Good." The older human leans back on the bench. "We still need to handle our side of this."

"What is your side of this? Exactly." Sacha asked.

"Our side, Miss, is the one that makes sure the town is safe from maniacs like Hines." He lowers his head a slight bit. "We don't have the resources you do. Finding him is going to be more challenging."

"I wouldn't say that." Ralph begins, "You have to understand that a man like this is looking for something. Glory. He wants credit or something that will give him riches, power. Things hunters don't need or usually want."

"From what we've seen, you're right. Few of us can do much about it." The man nods. "If you find him, let us know."

"As long as the information stream runs in both directions." Ralph adds.

"Agreed."

** *** **

A week easily passes, then two, before training resumes in a modified location. During that period of time, they continue to gather information on Jacob Hines, and when possible, on Tasha as well. Although she is more elusive, by the time the knight and his apprentices meet again in an obscure area of James' family farm, they know everything they need to about Hines, and the hunters he worked closest with.

Ralph settles against a stack of hay while James and Cerita finish their combat practice. Sacha sips on a bottle of water nearby. She asks, "They don't hold back do they?"

"Nope. Once she got the point of not doing so, I couldn't stop her, and that meant he had to step up. It's been pretty intense since." Ralph starts to fidget with a loose piece of hay that's sticking at him through his jeans.

"Then they are good for each other." She shifts close enough to lean on the haystack with Ralph.

"When do they stop?"

"Usually, when one needs medical attention." He looks over at her and smiles. "Sound familiar?"

She laughs. "Exactly how we like things. How long you think this round'll go?"

He focuses on the pair as Cerita blocks one of James' crossbow-bolts with her sword before stepping in toward him with her dagger. He deflects with a dagger of his own, and then slides his foot behind hers.

Quickly, forcefully, he leans forward pushing her shoulder back, and pulling her foot out from under her. Keeping her head from hitting the ground by dropping with her, and sliding his knees behind her head, he takes the opportunity to hold a dagger in her face.

"Halt," Ralph commands. The knight looks to Sacha. "That's a good spot."

His apprentices look at him, both winded. On command, they stop fighting. James helps her to her feet, and they begin to withdraw their armor and prepare their weapons. It only takes them a few moments before they join the master knights.

Sacha commends them, "I'm impressed. Both of you are very good, and getting better."

Cerita mutters, "He caught me off guard with the last one. Can't let that happen again."

Sacha smiles. "Maybe your next combat training should be against people you don't fight very often. Mikayla and Calinda would be thrilled to practice with someone else."

"Yeah." James runs his hand through his longer hair. "Calinda's . . . spirited."

"Yep. Even in her fighting." Sacha glances at Ralph, then back to the apprentices. "Right now they are checking on things back home, but should return shortly for duty."

Both apprentices nod.

"Speaking of which," Ralph stands a bit taller. "Hines and his goons are still in hiding, which means we know exactly where they are. Atlantis would like me to bring them back. Our task is obvious. We apprehend them before they cause more problems."

"What about the local police department? How will they handle this?" Cerita lifts a leg forward and begins to pull at the calf to stretch. "Won't they come after us for interference with a case or some such thing like that?"

James reminds her, "Your armor will keep that from happening. They won't be able to trace you, DNA or otherwise."

"Their technology is far too limited. Even the local hunters are better prepared." Sacha turns to Ralph. "You mentioned the hunter leader said something about their positions?"

"Yes. The hunters have been able to prove the murders of Kendra's family were Jacob Hines and Mathew Fuller. I've been assured the local police will have enough evidence to prove the same, even if they are unable to locate them after this evening."

"What happens to their place among the hunter's society stuff?" Cerita stretches the other leg.

"I avoid such questions. What goes on within their, whatever you want to call it, is on them." Ralph sighs. "Both of you shower, rest, and be ready to move in tonight. This is your first official mission. Make sure you're ready to follow directions exactly."

"Yes, sir."

** *** **

After Cerita is done showering she gets a visual communication from Atlantis. She activates it while she's still in her robe. Carlos's image hovers over her desk, where she has her cuff. "Hey, what's up?"

He sits on the chair behind the desk in his suites in Atlantis. His face is serious. "You know how we talked about a lot of things changing?"

"Yep. A few times now. Something else change?"

He nods. "Of course. I think dad'll give you more when you're home next though."

"Okay." She pronounces each sound carefully. "Are you okay?"

He nods again. "Yeah. I will be. I am, really just getting used to the news. I'm not supposed to talk about it much." He pauses before asking, "Can we just catch up?" He fidgets with a long string on his sleeve.

"Of course." She finds a shirt and steps out of viewing range to get dressed. "So, I've got my first official mission tonight." As she pulls her pants on, she explains, "I still don't know what it is, exactly, but it'll take a couple of teams."

"That sounds cool. Bet it'll be fun."

As she steps back into view, she shrugs. "I don't know. Maybe. Have to find out what it is, exactly, first." She spins to face her brother again. "It certainly won't be boring. How's school?"

"Slow." He heaves a sigh that can be seen. "You know how they were moving me into High School math classes and some science stuff like that too?"

"Yeah."

Carlos leans forward on his elbows on the desk. "I've been put in classes they consider remedial. Guess I didn't learn as much as a third grader down here."

"Bummer."

"Yep. Big one." Carlos pulls at a stray hair. "Oh, and mom isn't pushing the hair cut thing. Guess I'll have to get one myself. Maybe I could come get it done at the mall, like the last time. Without the green tips though."

"Maybe. I know mom's been really busy too." Cerita plops down on the bed. Her eyes locate the socks she pulled out before her shower. Making a note of where she dropped them, she returns her attention to her brother. "Have you had a few minutes to ask her about it?"

"Nope. When I'm not in school, I'm in 'learn noble etiquette' with an elf or dad. Or meeting more of the noble kids. Not too many are my age. At least not too many around for whatever these party things are."

"Sounds boring."

"It is." Carlos says flatly. "I stayed up the other night just to play video games. No time anywhere else in the day to play." His brow scrunches. "Do you know they don't have video games here?"

Cerita laughs. "Really? No one?"

He shakes his head hard. "Nope. It's so strange. It's like fun isn't really the same here."

"Have you met the goblins?" Cerita looks at him.

"Not yet. Supposed to meet them next week. I think. Soon." He shrugs.

"Okay so, ask them about it. They usually know about the surface stuff. I'd bet you'll find a goblin or more that know about the video games you play." Cerita yawns. "Ugh. I guess my workout wiped me. I should nap."

"Yeah. Everything here does that." He shakes his head again, then places both hands on his face. "Guess you should go."

"Hey, Carlos."

"Yeah?"

"It'll get better. Promise." She looks directly at the projection of her brother. "We'll get used to all of this."

"I know." He rubs his face and sighs again. "Just want to be over this new stuff already."

"Me too." She yawns again. "Hey, give mom and the little ones hugs for me, please."

"I will."

"Oh, and start a video journal. It'll do you some good." Cerita yawns one more time. "It's like vlogging, but doesn't have to be public. Vent away."

He laugh watching his sister fall asleep on him. "G'night, Cerita."

His hand extends across the table and shuts off his connection. He resolves to contact his sister the next morning to check on how her mission went.

From all that he's heard about her job and stuff, he's happy they trust her and James so much this fast. It's proof she's as good as he knows she is at everything she does.

Not that he'll ever tell her that part.

** *** **

Evening brings the knights and guides together again, rested and prepared. They stand in the shadows behind a large warehouse near the riverfront. Sacha reviews the armor of all four apprentices assembled. She is looking for any flaws or concerns that could prove problematic. She works both quickly and throughally.

Chandra takes James and Calinda into the building the moment they are cleared by Sacha. Together they sneak in to assess the situation. The warehouse is large and wide open.

Few things are scattered in the storage areas and the offices are all clustered in the same general two areas. It doesn't take them long to find four of the men inside offices on the north end of the building, but Jacob isn't with them.

She gestures to Calinda to search the south offices, and to James to search the lower level. Locating one man should be straightforward enough to be safe for the guides to separate. She keeps her eyes on the group already assembled from the darkened room across the hall.

The sounds of their hushed whispering carries clearly to her sensitive wercat ears. Talk of weapons cleaning and preparation remains the focus of their discussions. She hears murmurs about facing the head hunter, Edward, when this is over. It's then, that she realizes they are expecting the Atlanteans. Before she can call the apprentices back, she hears Calinda scream. Adrenaline rushes through her as both her maternal instincts and her duty move her to action.

She marks the room the four hunters are in before charging down the hall toward the sound of her daughter's scream.

As she barrels through a pair of doors that open to the warehouse floor, she finds Calinda and James bound and together with Jacob Hines stalking around them. Blood pours down James' cheeks. Calinda is kicked hard in the abdomen before Chandra can land on her feet below.

She snarls.

"Ah, another pretty kitty comes to play." Jacob Hines laughs, grabs a fist full of Calinda's fur, and yanks her head back. "Aww, worried about the young ones. How sweet." He slams the girl's head into the large beam she's secured to. "Nothing to worry about. You're all going to die tonight."

Chandra stalks closer. "We'll see about that."

Noble Transition

Before she can reach Hines, an arrow flies past her head. She doesn't have to turn around to know the other hunters have joined the battle. She paces to her left, moving herself closer to Calinda as she does. The sound of a gunshot ricochets off the walls. She crouches low. Even in full armor, she's still vulnerable in places.

Hines pays almost no attention to Chandra. Instead, he moves to the center of the room, where he has the lanky elf tied up. Stooping down, he notices the blood on his face has started to recede, and his wounds are healing. He slaps the places that were cut hard enough to tear them open again. "Can't have you healing yet. Need to call that vampyre back here, too."

James doesn't cry out when struck. Instead of giving into the physical violence, he meditates. He finds the process both comforting and good for keeping the pain in control.

Jacob pulls the boy's hair back, out of his face and he appears to be sleeping. "Now, now, can't have you missing all of this. Let's see what we can do to wake you up, shall we?"

He withdraws his dagger again, and plunges it into the soft spot between the armor joints on one of his shoulders. Twisting it deeper, he forces it in far enough for the hilt to stop him. He withdraws faster than he forced it in.

James' eyes shoot open. Tears course down his cheeks, but not a sound carries from his mouth.

"That's better."

While Chandra tries to free her daughter, she's forced to turn away from the pain inflicted upon the elf. Her claws slash at the cable wiring holding her daughter's hands together, with no effect. Calinda attempts to pull away from her mother as a hunter gets close enough to strike. Chandra looks up to find a man with a small handgun pointed at her head. Without much thought, the woman kicks her leg out, knocking him down to one knee. The sudden shift in weight forces him to compress the trigger wildly.

The stray bullet flies above them, striking Sacha as she enters from the second level. The knight flinches when the bullet bounces off her armor. A moment later, she's over the railing and on the floor below, running after the hunter that fired the gun.

Ralph enters the building through the main doors on the floor to the warehouse. His sword is raised in his hand. "Hines."

The man looks at the master knight. "I was wondering when you'd arrive. The pretty kitties and lady were nice distractions, but your little trainee here," he kicks James in the side for emphasis, "has been very well behaved for me."

Blood spatters from James' mouth upon impact.

The sound of fighting is heard as Ralph approaches the man holding a dagger over his student. "You've done enough. I'm here."

"No, I've only just started." He laughs, slams the boy's head with his boot, and charges the knight. Instead of being impaled by the knight's blade, he spins, extends his dagger, and slices the knight's wrist at the only place he could. "Been practicing that one. Nice trick, huh?"

Ralph swings the sword in his strong hand. It lands hard on Jacob's thigh, but it leaves him open for the fist that comes crashing across his helmet.

The helmet vibrates briefly before the knight draws the hilt hard against on the gut of the former hunter. Hines doubles over, laughing.

Ralph puts both fists around the sword, and then slams the hilt on the back of the former hunter's head. This forces Hines' face into Ralph's knee. Blood begins to pour from Jacob Hines' nose, yet he continues to laugh. It only takes Ralph a moment to realize there is a slight pulsation that's unnatural to the battle emanating from his helmet. His sword clamors as it hits the ground.

The knight removes his helmet and throws it as far away from everything as he can, only to watch it explode before it makes contact with the ground again.

With the knight's face bare, the hunter brings his dagger up again, slicing into the man's head. Laughter is no longer heard as he relentlessly attacks the knight with one blow after another. Some are deflected, while others land squarely where he intends to strike. Ralph fights back with equal ferocity.

Sacha stands between two hunters. A crossbow is pointed at her head, and a gun is directed at her guide. Mikayla lays healing but unconscious, at the feet of a third hunter. Sacha doesn't spare a glance when she hears something explode behind her. It's all she can do to hope James survives.

"Drop your sword." A darker haired man commands her.

"So you can shoot me instead?" Sacha shakes her head. "I'm older than you look."

The bolt flies at her head, impacting her helmet hard at close range, which forces her to remove it in order to avoid the painful resonance. She can feel her face start to swell where the bolt struck through the helmet, but she knows skin isn't broken.

"Aw, this one's just a human. Do we have to kill her, or can we play first?" A redheaded man with a scruffy beard grins in her direction. "You like having fun right?"

She dips down, grabs her sword, and swings at his legs. "Mermaids don't have fun with scum."

He takes a step back and aims the gun at her. "You made a stupid choice. But first, let's kill the other knight, so she can't get back up." He takes aim at Mikayla, and Sacha is back on her feet with her sword through the man's abdomen.

She leans in on the gunman. "No one will take my daughter's life when I'm here."

The man's eyes open briefly before he collapses on the floor.

Sacha spins around, slicing wildly at the man with the crossbow.

He dodges, loads a bolt, and fires at Calinda, slicing through the thigh of her armor. She screams again.

Chandra scrambles again to free her daughter. As she moves, she is struck hard by the back of the crossbow at the base of her skull. Blood trickles, but she remains focused, albeit dazed. A large arm wraps around her neck and starts to pull her from the cable binding Calinda.

Sacha tackles the man. As she begins throwing armored punches at his face and chest, she hears a different man scream loudly. Her head jerks around to find Mikayla impaling the hunter standing over her.

When her face spins back to her own target, she finds a fist in her face. The crack that results sends sharp pain through her whole head.

She's grateful that her nanites continue to work to both heal her and make it less painful. She blocks much of the oncoming barrage of fists that force her to unpin him.

Before she regains balance, she sees her daughter's blade protruding through the front of the attacking former hunter.

He falls on top of Sacha.

She pushes his weight off, and pulls her daughter into a hug.

Sacha kicks the sword into Chandra's reach, which allows her to finally free Calinda.

The four take a moment to breathe as they watch the battle between Ralph and Jacob Hines.

Cerita slides next to James. Quietly placing her bag next to him, she wipes the dried blood from his face. When he doesn't respond, she is overcome with tears. "Oh, please be okay. Please let your nanites work."

She slips her dagger from her bag and begins cutting away at the wire holding him. *Arms first and then legs.* She keeps her thoughts on the moment and what she's been trained to do. Before she can cut through his legs, an arrow impacts her arm from behind. She looks to find someone standing in the shadows. The bow targets her again. This time, she pulls her dagger back and is able to prevent it from digging into her arm. She cries out, "We were trying to help."

Another arrow flies in her direction. This time, it strikes James in the bare hand. He groans.

Cerita withdraws her sword from her side, and activates her armor. "Stop it!" In moments, she's in the armor that encompassed her during the Choosing. As another arrow flies toward her, her armor deflects it in activation. She lifts her sword and stands over James. "What do you want?"

Not a word is uttered as the raven haired girl steps from the shadows. The bow is drawn again, this time the tip of the arrow is thin, metal, and turning red. The arrow is released and it slices through Cerita's armor. The girl smirks.

Cerita pulls the arrow from her abdomen and instantly she regrets it. Blood begins to pool in her armor.

She can feel her medical nanobots doing their job, but the pain is still intense. Her eyes blink back tears, while her sword deflects another arrow. *Stay focused, and let the medi bots do their thing.*

The girl steps closer still, this time aiming for James, clearly aware she has something that can penetrate his armor too. The arrow is loosed, and another is loaded before the last can impact.

Cerita pushes James out of the way of the arrow, only to have it pierce her arm instead. When she returns her focus to the girl again, she barely deflects the next arrow. Only a step further, and Kendra is standing at the other end of the bow, pointing the arrow at her chest. Cerita desperately asks, "Why are you doing this?"

Kendra's gaunt face grins. "Because you should never count humans out."

"I don't. I'm human, remember?" Cerita keeps her sword raised, her mind focused on the task, and her breathing as steady as she's able.

"You are *nothing*. You align yourself with those who would kill us, control us, or worse." She sneers and pulls the bow a bit tighter. "Traitors will die."

"But I'm not the traitor. He is." She gestures toward Hines still locked in battle with Ralph. "He killed your family."

"Do you think I don't know that? I was there and told him how to do it." She leans her face a little closer to the shaft of the arrow, so her eye was trailing down the end to its target.

A light seems to dance in Kendra's eyes. "I can't miss from here. Any last words?"

Cerita lowers the point of her sword. She takes a deep breath and whispers, "I'm sorry I couldn't save you."

A moment later, Kendra doubles over, grasping a smaller arrow in her abdomen. Her eyes drop to James, whose aim couldn't have missed at this distance either. "Well done." In seconds, she collapses.

Cerita falls to her knees next to the elf. Tears of relief stream down her face. He reaches a hand up and brushes them away.

James whispers, "Shh, it's over."

Cerita nods and leans forward, placing her forehead on his. "Yeah." They sit there for several minutes looking at each other, happy to be alive and together. "I hope we don't do that again soon."

He closes his eyes. "Me too."

As she helps him lean back on the floor to rest. Their attention moves to the action continuing in the back of the large room.

A light flashes brightly. A grunt is heard, blades impact, and finally, silence.

Ralph kneels, breathing heavily. It takes him several minutes to recover before assessing where his team is, or what had been accomplished.

Over the next several hours, the small team recovers from the battle, and begins to cleanse the area of all traces of their struggle. Kendra is moved to Atlantis, and placed in a cell near Jacob's. The room is flooded with medical bots to tend her wounds. Those who died in the fight are taken offworld, through Atlantis, for burial. Before the sun rises in the morning, the only traces of the struggle left behind are in the lingering wounds of the Atlanteans.

** *** **

Carlos settles at his desk and attempts to reach his sister again. With his mother so busy, Cerita is the only person he can rely on for a normal conversation. When she doesn't respond, he becomes worried. A servant enters the room. "Find my father," he demands.

The servant responds, "I can not do that, sire. There are more pressing matters the council is attending right now."

"What is more pressing than I am? I'm his son!"

The elfin man steps further into the room and secures the door firmly. "I am not privileged to such information. Perhaps your mother would be of assistance."

Carlos shakes his head. "She won't know," he grumbles.

"Won't know what, sire?" The servant sits next to the boy.

The young man sighs. "Won't know if my sister is okay."

"Is there a reason she would not be, young sire?" the servant's face scrunches with concern.

"She had a mission yesterday. Last night. I just tried to reach her. She didn't answer." He looks at the man who's helped him a lot since he arrived. "Is that normal?"

"If her mission was in the evening, it is possible she is resting." The servant folds his hands together.

"You're right." He pauses. "It is."

"In that case, sire, she would be fine."

"Yep." Carlos's face seems to grow longer. "What is on the agenda for today? Do I get some video game time?"

"You have a task this afternoon, sire. Two more families to meet." The elf clears his throat. "There is preparation required. You'll need to learn new language introductions."

"How many more of these are there?" Carlos grumbles. He's met eight different noble houses. He knows once he's met them all, he has to accept something he's not sure he'll ever be ready to accept.

"There are two more meetings, sir. Once you've met them, you'll move into the next phase of your preparation." The dark haired elfin man stands and approaches Carlos. "It will be a smooth transition."

"I'm sure it will be. It's still going to be hard." He looks up at the man with him. "You sure there's a lot of others doing this?"

"I'm here specifically to prepare you, as I've done with others. I promise, everything is as I've said. I'll make the transfer with you, when the time comes."

Carlos stands. "Do I have to dress up again?"

The elf nods. "Always."

"Ugh." The boy drops his head and moves without much motivation to the bedroom. After several minutes he emerges again in far more elaborate clothing than just his jeans and t-shirt. His smooth white tunic, and soft cream slacks are accented by his golden skin. "This work?"

"Yes, sir." The elf lowers his head. "Should we begin rehearsing your greetings?"

"I guess." The boy sits in the sitting area. "Promise me something."

"What would you like me to promise, sire?"

"Promise I will have a visit from the younger ones after we transfer to the new location."

"You have my word, sire. I will do everything within my ability and authority to ensure you visit your family as often as possible. I also promise when it is possible, the reverse will occur as well."

Carlos nods. "Thanks, Josh."

Noble Transition

Epilogue

On the mainland, a man in a dark leather jacket with soft brown colored hair strolls generously behind the redheaded vampyress. A cell phone is pressed to his ear, and he whispers into it. "She found them."

The voice on the other end inquires, "Does she know you're there?"

"I haven't seen any evidence she does, or would." His eyes narrow as she turns off the direct path in the grassy park. "Then again, she might. We'll see."

"Don't let her find you until we have finished preparing."

"Of course, my king."

"Check in with me if anything changes."

"Yes, Sire." He pauses his step, glances toward the direction she seems to have turned, but sees no further movement. "I will reach you again soon. Goodnight, your highness."

"Goodnight, Romeo."

Noble Transition

From the Author

It's fantastic you've made it through book three. There's a lot that's happened.

Cerita discovered her family isn't what she expected in book one. Book two she faced death and won. In book three she introduced her family to her father and the world she's become a part of, and she and Carlos are adjusting with some obstacles they didn't expect. But then, do you think learning a whole new history is something that could be anticipated? What about new skills? Both of the newly found Blocc children are growing their new skills as quickly as those around them can teach them.

What do you think of this Forsaken business? Seems worrisome if someone is looking for the Atlanteans.

What are you enjoying about the series so far? Join us for conversation and discussion on our facebook page and at my Knight's page on my website. There's so much fun going on and growing.

When we hit book 6 – watch for the omnibus to follow. I'll make sure to include a glossary, reader's guide, and more goodies for you to enjoy. If there's a request, please don't hesitate to let leave me a message and I'll see what I can add to the final season release.

And as a bonus – I want you to watch for Carlos's upcoming series release. I'll have an excerpt and announcement details on my site soon.

Can't wait to talk to you!

Catrina Taylor
CatrinaTaylor.com
Facebook.com/KnightsoftheImmortals

Noble Transition

Midnight Rose Titles

By Author KG Stutts
New Adult Scifi Romance
Mirror Series – Mirror Image, Mirror Shattered, and Mirror Reformed.
Amethyst Chronicles Volume 1
Mirror Origins Shorts

By Author Tiana Lebeau
Contemporary Lives Books
Shattered Lives and Alone – Undefeated

By Author Samai'a
Children's Book Series – You Finish It